LIFE POSTPONED

Life Postponed

MARK TAYAR

madnest.org

Life Postponed

By Mark John Tayar

Proudly published independently by MadNest in Sydney, Australia on December 1, 2020.

Copyright © Mark John Tayar 2020
Author: Tayar, Mark John
Category: Contemporary Fiction
ISBN (Print): 978-0-6450492-0-6
ISBN (Ebook): 978-0-6450492-1-3

Related Publications by Dr Mark Tayar

Tayar, M. J. and Tayar, M. E. (2020). *The Journey Beyond Psychosis: Australian Research, Stories & Resources*. Sydney, available for free at tayar.com.au/journey

Tayar, M. J. and Tayar, M. E. (2019). *Managing Psychosis: an Australian Guide*. Bloomington: Xlibris.

Image Credits

Photographs and graphics all royalty free from Pixabay with modifications by Mark Tayar. Cover image by Nam Nguyen (namair), Tree drawing adapted from digital illustration by Annalise Batista (AnnaliseArt), Arm background image by Keifit, Chalkboard background image by Stux. Icons all royalty free and modified from freepik.

Content Warning / Trigger Warning

NB: *Some people may find parts of this novel confronting or distressing, especially those with lived experience of psychiatric wards, drug use, suicidal ideation or bereavement from suicide. Take care.*

*To all those survivors of the mental health
system and to those we lost too early.*

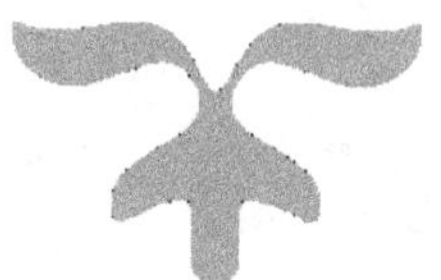

Acknowledgements

I acknowledge the ideas, basic editing and afterword provided by my mum Margaret Tayar to gain a better understanding of the perspective of a carer or support person. I thank Raymond Chow for his proofreading, feedback and many years of close support.

I thank all those consumers, carers and clinicians who shared their stories with me and helped progress my own journey from illness to recovery and renewal.

I also deeply and respectfully acknowledge the Cabrogal clan of the great Darug nation from the lands where this book was written. This always was and always will be Aboriginal land with sovereignty never ceded. First Nations approaches to fostering better social, emotional, spiritual and cultural wellbeing need to be much better documented, understood and incorporated in culturally appropriate ways. The resilience, strength and wisdom of Australian Aboriginal and Torres Strait Islanders as well other First Nation cultures like that of Māori people in New Zealand have immense unrealised potential to foster better health in our region.

Preface

Mental health challenges often put a temporary hold on life. This doesn't necessarily mean cancelling everything but rather postponing life or creating something new. In 2020, we all experienced 'cancel culture' and almost everyone felt some form of mental distress from the chaos of lock down. For many people confined to psych wards in 2020, doors were constantly locked to patients except if they were discharged from the hospital.

Visitors were limited to certain times in Australian psych wards or not allowed at all. Many visitors just stayed away due to the rational fear that hospitals harbour infection. In the largest state of NSW, the number of hospital visitors per day was limited to just one but this was still better than the zero visitors allowed by NSW prisons for most of 2020. Some mental health patients were discharged faster because of additional funds for group homes or because they were at higher risk of COVID-related complications.

The central stories in this book are based on real events in Sydney but not in 2020 and not with any patients I have worked with professionally. Names, locations and other identifying details of stories have been changed slightly for privacy, confidentiality and respect for those involved. The details have been taken from my time as a patient, not as a healthcare worker but some details on health systems are understood from real work experiences. Personal experiences from 2016-2019 are recontextualised to the pandemic conditions with new pressures and opportunities for change arising in 2020. Themes related to Australian Aboriginal people have been used in consultation with relevant members of these communities but future work is needed for First Nations people with mental health challenges to tell their own stories.

Given the level of authenticity of these stories, people who have gone through psych wards or supported those who have may be retraumatised by this content. The patient experiences do not comprise a large portion of the three main narratives but there are some themes such as suicidality that many may find confronting. If this is the case, please postpone your reading, do some self-care and reach out to professionals or resources on the United for Global Mental Health website (quick link at: tayar.com.au/h). Some skills for managing distress are explained in this book.

After reading, please also share your own story if it is safe to do so. This means sharing stories without harming your reputation in terms of risks like losing your job or sharing your story in a way that retraumatises others. Resources on 'safe storytelling' can help this process and many of these principles have been followed in this novel except where engagement with traumatic details are important to understand the extent of issues and how to deal with them.

The aim of *Life Postponed* is to show what it's really like to live with chronic mental illness and be incarcerated in a psych ward against your will but gradually recover. For some, it's not recovery but growth then renewal while others always retain most parts of their former identity but with ongoing symptoms. Mental health recovery journeys are different for everyone but there are some universals explored here. Recovery often comes with relapse and sometimes rehospitalisation. Rather than a cure, the concept of recovery here refers to living well despite ongoing symptoms and ongoing traumatic memories of past symptoms.

Health systems in Australia and to a greater extent in many other countries were stress-tested with each major wave of COVID-19. In parallel to the strains in medical wards of large hospitals, there were different challenges introduced to psych wards in the same hospitals or elsewhere. There were viral infections spreading within health systems as well as a viral-like spreading of anxiety, trauma and psychosis exacerbated by lockdown stress, the effects of infection on the brain, or increased substance use.

No life is immune from being postponed or cancelled by mental distress.

~ 1 ~

ONE

In Sydney's inner-west, a young man screamed in his two-storey home. Billy had an unusual day and was not screaming at people, just restless and wanting to get his thoughts out. He didn't sleep the night before and instead wandered round his leafy suburban neighbourhood.

Billy was used to not sleeping when a new idea came into his head for a new application or website. He could rarely focus on the latest idea for an app but kept coding and changing things with a quick thrill as every new idea came in. He only went out for a walk to try and clear his head but things around him seemed like signs that sparked ideas which he quickly typed into his phone with abbreviations and themes later hard to interpret.

Billy lived with his parents who were born in British-controlled Hong Kong. They noticed that their son had been a little off lately. As a geek, Billy always did behave differently to their two daughters to the extent that strange behaviours often went unnoticed by Joy and Henry. Billy had recently finished up pretty well at school in maths and two technology subjects but didn't want to go to uni because of an interest in making money quickly in software coding then maybe starting his own business.

In his walk around dimly lit local streets he met randoms who seemed like they were paid actors or some other kind of imposters. This was a new kind of suspicion and the underlying logic for it was unclear.

As well as making notes in his phone, he carried a small notepad around the streets that night and scribbled down parts of software code. The code seemed to come to life on the page. It looked as if it was flowing naturally but changing directions like a river -derived from a source high above and flowing into something big.

Yelling helped to get out thoughts out like he was expelling them from his body but then they were somehow embedded into the universe to then bounce back as an even better idea. The assemblages of ideas and patterns brought a new dimension to Billy's world. The once parallel essences of life started to intersect and interlace.

Trying to explain this to others was near impossible. Were Billy's parents and his sister unenlightened or actively working against him like those at work and the imposters around the neighbourhood? Billy's screaming started up again:

"What am I meant to be doing? What impact do you want me to have'? FUUCCCK!!"

Billy noticed his face was much warmer like when he was forced into public speaking. His heart was beating like a drum circle -random but with a curious rhythm. He had never been on meds before, but Billy knew if he was too open about his recent realisations, someone might tranquilise or sedate him.

A jarring knock on his bedroom door startled Billy. He had a new sense of auditory sensitivity not felt before -even worse than sensitivity from light and sound during a harsh hangover.

Henry entered and asked: "R U all-right?" having seen that on the back of a phonebooth. "I'm Fine" is the reply but with a stare like someone had switched off his WiFi connection to the rest of the world.

As the first light of dawn snuck in through a slit in his curtains, it was like the WiFi reconnected. He realised it was Thursday and he had work in two hours. The shower water hit the bathroom tiles in a way that echoed unlike he had experienced before and sounded like someone whispering. His heart beat unusually and in tandem with a noticeably different pattern of the rise and fall of his lean chest.

Thinking about his day ahead Billy spoke to himself, "Is work part of my bigger purpose? Will there be signs and symbols there to point to where this rapid flow of ideas was feeding into?"

He put on his favourite V-neck tee over a lean body. He chose the shirt because it was dark blue like the ocean. With black jeans and casual canvas shoes, Billy gave the 'not now' look as he sped past three of his family members eating brekkie. For Joy and Henry, it was congee but their son and daughter still living at home, the standard cereal and toast was out for them to have with instant coffee.

On the train, his Day Mix music stream seemed a bit different to normal. The algorithm had corrected slightly based on what he was listening to while on the prowl in Strathfield late last night. Major Lazer's collab with Justin Bieber played:

> Everyone gets high sometimes...And if you feel you're sinking, I will jump right over into cold, cold water for you... I won't let go I'll be your lifeline tonight... You shouldn't be fighting on your own.

Though only really being a closet 'Belieber', listening to this song from four years ago was like it was chosen by someone else. Maybe a tech company was trying to intervene in Billy's life. Perhaps the myth was true that Chinese-government affiliated phone manufactures left back doors into devices like his. Another explanation could be a higher power creating coincidences in order to send Billy messages about his life mission.

"Arhhh pbhh, I'm trippin again" Billy seemed to say in his head but a few people on the socially-undistanced train turned and stared like it was audible to them. COVID-19 had just started to really infect the mindset of everyday Sydneysiders but not yet the behaviour.

"I'm not from fucking Wuhan, stop looking at me" said Billy to one of the train passengers.

It sounded like one of the other passengers was talking about a 'skinny Asian gayboy' -maybe it was about him. Was his XS shirt getting tighter with all the recent stress-eating making him look gay? Another rando was listening to 'If the world was ending' which a second later shuffled onto Billy's Day Mix – a coincidence or a message?

"If the world was ending, no one would come over to my 'COVID-safe bubble' right now." thought Billy with a lonely sadness.

Songs that seemed to explore a paradox of tragedy and hope all played consecutively and Billy appreciated the lyrics with newly discovered apparent subtext.

"Fuck, at Wynyard -must have spaced when we stopped at Town Hall" realised Billy to himself. All good though, he would just cut through the tunnels of Barangaroo, head back through Darling Harbour and go across the bridge to his work around the piers of Pyrmont.

At work, he stared at all the free cereal and couldn't decide which one would maximise flavour and energy for the morning. The chocolatey one maybe but he suddenly lost his appetite.

'R U all-right?' asked Billy's colleague. "Not that question again, are people bloody gaslighting me today?" thought Billy referring to manipulation that makes you think you are crazy which can be intentional or unintentional.

He replied "Fine, thanks Allie, just indecisive today". Maybe getting that question twice in one day was a sign of something intensely wrong or a sign something even worse was on the horizon. Most people still don't ask the question though and when they do, it can sound like an unhelpful proxy for the judgement that "you are acting weird".

After that delay through Barangaroo where the new casino was being built and a quick journey across the water to where the old casino is, Friday the 13th felt like an ironically great day to gamble. That might be a good reward at lunch after five hours of programming the next version of his company's flagship enterprise database software. Just a quick slap on the poker machines at the casino -maybe just $13 to stick his finger up at the superstitions of Black Friday.

Coding was always a bit of a rush and breaks just seemed pointless on the average day but today Billy coded straight from 8am-4pm. Running checks on his code, there were a lot more errors than usual but he was getting so much done and it was like geek crack. Allie noticed the hardstyle music out of Billy's headphones a bit louder and with higher BPM than normal.

"How many lines of code did you get through today mate?" Allie asked expecting about 30 debugged lines of code (LOC) as usual. "61 LOC and counting Al" was the reply. Billy felt at the same time full of energy mentally but totally drained physically after all the walking last night. He rushed to the vending machine for an energy drink with a feeling that 2 cans would be OK "cos they were zero-sugar".

Billy clocked off at 7pm and went straight to the nearby casino. His eyes must have been really red because casino security asked if he had taken anything. Normally they don't give a crap, but they seemed vaguely concerned that Billy might make a scene on the gaming floor.

"Just a long day mate, you'd know what that's like with your work right?" which of course he did and with that false empathy, Billy was in. He bought and quickly drunk another two guarana drinks but with a shot of vodka each -it was Friday after all. Billy did not think of himself as a typical Asian IT loner but was quite comfortable being there by himself and talked to any hardcore gambler who made eye contact or otherwise seemed friendly.

"Dude, how many of those vodka energy drinks have you had? You playing that machine fast" said a handsome surfie-type on the next machine.

"All good, just putting 10c bets totalling $13 on each machine cos it's Friday the 13th. Like a good-luck system but focusing on bad luck or something, haha" explained Billy in a creepy way. The surfie guy raised his eyebrows and went back to his game.

"Gotta get some smokes" Billy said rapidly as he collected his remaining 80c to escape the awkwardness of the interaction with the surfie. Billy didn't normally smoke but started again the previous night after thinking smoking was a good way to meet new people waiting around in outside areas. He was generous giving out smokes to those who asked but this was just an amplification of his usual generosity -not out-of-control wastage.

With each drag of the cigarette, the racing thoughts slowed down slightly on the inhale and disappeared totally on the exhale. It was like doing the mindfulness of breath activities that he learned at his pretentious high school. Probably weed would slow the thoughts down to a more manageable speed but it made Billy super paranoid usually.

"Crap, I didn't sanitise those last four pokies before touching them. Didn't use the sanitiser before scratching my nose either. Maybe I've infected the next people playing the same pokies or that surfie. Ah, we haven't had many new cases in the state, I'll be fine" thought Billy in a quick string of thoughts that would soon become everyday concerns of many people throughout the world.

When looking around all the Asian faces in the casino, Billy was still conscious of the xenophobic bullshit of American politicians focusing on Wuhan to mirror and then intensify public perceptions of all Asians as infected. Walking out a casino with just a net loss of $44, he felt pretty safe from potential racist abuse. There are many East Asian people around Darling Square and Central where he walked through sometimes to get a quick meal for dinner and then catch a train back to his family's home.

What was more noticeable and unsettling than usual in this walk was all the cameras with their little flashing red lights and semi-spherical covers partially obscuring which direction the filming was focused on. He hadn't done anything wrong but there was just a stronger sense that Big Brother was watching. This seemed linked to an inevitable knee-jerk attempt by the government at greater surveillance to track new infections.

Along the old trainline now a nice pathway and past the television studios, Billy wondered if certain people walking past were spying on him. Then, walking through the 300 metre Devonshire Street Tunnel to get to his train platform, all the people in a small space made him feel very edgy. The humidity in that tunnel, the fluoro lights and ghastly murals overloaded Billy's senses so he sped up to the pace of a hardstyle remix of The Middle playing in his overly expensive headphones.

Even with the noise cancelling of the headphones playing fairly loud music, he thought he heard people in the tunnel talk about him. He could hear them say things about his body, his sexuality, his dress sense and how he looked really tired. More alcohol was clearly a bad choice in response to this but might numb things enough to last the train ride back without being so paranoid.

Up through Surry Hills, the first two corner pubs seemed a bit dodgy. Then up at Crown Street the bars there seemed too wanky. Oxford Street wasn't that far so he decided to 'gay it up'. Billy wasn't into 'the scene' of the gay strip of Darlinghurst but knew he could have a dance until quite late with fast music and a decent crowd. He felt a bit more up for a hook-up than usual and either a gay/bi guy or a straight/bi girl would be fine for some ego-boosting attention and maybe an overnighter at their place.

The music on the top floor of Stonewall was usually a lot faster than the other two levels so Billy stumbled up the stairs. He got two vodka lemonades as he was already a bit shaky from all the caffeine. The bartender was friendly but still gave an odd look and commented something to the other bartender. Was he going to call security?

On the dance floor, Billy tried some new muzzing styles as well as the jerky actions of the hakken style that got a giggle from a Hen's party seated nearby. He gently grabbed the hand of the bride-to-be and instructed her through a sexier version of the old school Melbourne shuffle. Then they switched to a synchro rave step as he placed his left foot back, right foot forward in a mirrored sequence with her like a hardcore Hokey Pokey (Hokey Cokey).

"Why are you shaking so much?" the Hen asked. "Not sure, probably all the caffeine or maybe it's a hectic new dance style!" joked Billy back.

After 11 more drinks, security came. "What have you taken mate? How many pills have you had? Wait here while the police come" said a large security guard who seemed a bit out of place for a gay bar. Speeding down the stairs while ordering a ride share, security couldn't touch him. "Fuck, 9 minutes for the ride share to get here, better leg it to a back street and get them to follow his GPS" thought Billy as he walked quickly to backstreets without running so as not to attract attention.

Into a graffiti-filled lane behind a sex toy shop and men-only sauna. Maybe he could go to the gay sauna to get a release from this drama of stress and paranoia or maybe a new sex toy would be safer and less awkward.

Sirens blared as Billy thought, "Mustn't be for me, haven't done anything wrong."

"Stop mate!" screamed one of four coppers getting out of a white van. "Were you just at Stonewall buddy?" said the burly female cop. "Unless I've done something wrong, where I have been tonight is private" asserted Billy. "It's not what you did, it's just some things you said. We think it might be good to get you to hospital" said the Sergeant.

Still feeling full of energy and knowing he wasn't under arrest, Billy just said "no, thanks" and sprinted but into a dead-end lane. The cops waddled quickly in pursuit. "This is part of my mission" thought Billy. "All cops are bastards and I need to stand up to this bullying" he planned dangerously.

With no intention of being violent, this young slim Australian-born Chinese man exclaimed: "I haven't done anything wrong, leave this lane now and I will go home peacefully." A drag queen walked along an intersecting street and in a deep voice said, "he is an unarmed skinny little twink, take a few steps back please!"

One officer put his hand on his taser reminding Billy of a death eight years ago the next suburb over caused by police taser. Billy took a special interest in the case when signing a petition about taser use. He recalled parts of the exact Coroner's findings of that terrible incident: "Go on, taser me and see if you can beat your mate's record of seven times in a minute." The police moved forward in unison with the drag queen screaming. Billy was tackled and then quickly restrained on the ground with unnecessary force considering his build and lack of any threat of violence.

~ 2 ~

TWO

Billy muttered to himself in the back of the police van. He could just hear parts of what the police were saying. It seemed to be about him and terrible things that might happen to him at the hospital. There are no beds at the psych ward closest to Darlinghurst, but they still took him to the closest Emergency Department (ED).

The police escorted him to an interview room in a hospital that seemed familiar but had a weird setup. He asked about the cameras, requested that no one contact his parents and said he didn't have any injuries so should not be in ED. An obese Middle Eastern-looking security guard and a nurse entered the room as the coppers left.

"What's going on, have I been in a COVID hotspot? Do I have COVID? Where is the swabbing thing? Were the police watching me on the cameras all day? Who knows I'm here?" asked Billy in such rapid succession that it was difficult for the Registered Nurse (RN) to understand. The quick talking seemed to reflect the flight of ideas common in manic phases of diagnoses like bipolar I and schizoaffective disorder but there was not going to be any specific diagnosis that night.

Three old TVs hanging from the ED ceiling were tuned to news blaring that: "confirmed cases have doubled every three days surging from less than 200 to more than 2,000 within the last 12 days." All the chaos of an ED also now included new fears of a bigger surge into hospitals and possible infection while in hospital. Perhaps a chilled music video station would be preferable to news in this setting.

A very young Indian-looking lady came in. "What is your name, date of birth and suburb?" she said without a proper greeting or any sign of emotion.

"Billy, ahhh, why do I have to tell you this? It's March 20, 1999 and I live in North Strathfield so if I need to be in hospital please get me a bed near there."

"Well, there's no psych beds here so you will probably get what you want." Dr Bina the junior Psychiatry Registrar replied.

'What do you mean psych bed? I just need some water and sleep to sober up' which fell on deaf ears but is a conviction Billy held for six more hours in emergency with no one telling him what is going on. With a second night of no sleep, things started getting even more strange than in the tunnel under Central Station.

A young feminine male nurse occasionally came past and checked blood pressure and heart rate. Billy was tachycardic with a heart rate of 143 BPM -similar to the speed of his favourite the Dutch hardstyle. The machine measuring this just made Billy more intensely anxious and it ticked up higher whenever he looked at the number.

"Have you been smoking or injecting ice Billy?" said the passive aggressive assistant nurse. "Fuck no, fuck off!" was the reply. A patient on the other side of the ED grumbled "not another bloody psycho junkie."

Billy is then asked to go to an area called PECC. The large room looked like most other hospitals with curtained off beds for eight people. Nurses in a room overlooking the beds were surrounded by thick acrylic plastic like bullet proof glass. The nurses behind the glass can see you and you can see them talk to each other or sit on computers for extended periods. Waiting at the entrance to be told what to do takes forever so Billy knocked repeatedly on the glass but was totally ignored.

He banged on the glass, screamed and started yelling about cameras, Friday the 13th and coronavirus. The yelling got the nurses to finally shift out of their inertia. Loud beeping started, someone said 'code black' and two security guards in vests almost as thick as body armour restrained this 56kg adolescent. They stripped jeans and injected him in the bum with something. Having those security guards and nurses see his naked body felt so violating that he would retain the trauma of that memory for life. It was like a flock of seagulls around him in a feeding frenzy. Billy did not try and swat them away, but they still restrained and injected him while asking again if he was on ice.

Something was taped to his chest that feels like a bomb. In an overmedicated haze, Billy felt like his living nightmare had just got a lot worse. The meds settled him but he still moaned and tossed around for an hour then slept with nightmares of rioters and dead bodies in the street from Covid.

'Can you tell me what day it is Billy?' said an older nurse who entered a small room with just a bed. 'It's Saturday, who are you?'. 'Ah, lost a day have you? It's actually Sunday morning and we have brekkie ready for you' said the RN named Martha. 'Am I still at that Darlinghurst Hospital sorry?' said Billy with Martha replying 'nope, you're at your friendly local acute ward and your Dad will be here at the 11am visiting hour.'

Henry was only mildly worried about Billy not being a home ready for Saturday's brunch. His son had some all-nighters before but with the weird behaviour on Thursday made him more confused than anything. With the news of hospitalisation coming on Saturday, Henry was worried about how everything would affect his wife Joy and their two daughters. Mental illness was more accepted than before but being in a psych ward was still deeply shameful -especially for Chinese-background families like them even though they had been in Australia for decades.

Among family friends there was already talk about Billy being strange because of all his gaming and late-night dance parties. Then there were all the rumours about him being gay which turned out to be half-true. Henry was confident that the trip to hospital would quickly reveal a mix up and the doctors would soon realise his son was fine to leave.

In the ward of 20 beds of males and females, there was screaming, suspicious looks and a lot of co-patients pacing back and forth. Billy felt like everyone there was actually really sick, and he was fine.

He looked out a window and recognised it as being a hospital a few suburbs away from his place. It was nice to be close to home, but he then checked all the doors and windows. He was completely locked in.

Some forms and leaflets were on a small desk on his room but he was so drowsy and confused. One had legalistic rubbish about 'Schedule 3A' which may as well as been in Traditional Chinese -a language he could recognise but had little meaning and felt totally foreign. He defaulted to his teenage obsession with computers and current work in IT to ask for a tablet computer or web kiosk to get in touch with friends and family.

There were no computers available and his phone was placed in a locker that he was an 'Involuntary Patient' could not access until 'escorted leave' was approved by his 'Consultant' which would be the case even if he was 'Voluntary'. Again, may as well have been in Chinese and who the hell would volunteer to be locked up in such a place?

"Breakfast!" announced a chubby lady wheeling a large case with doors on each side. There were trays with each patient's full name on it.

"I could out any of these people as insane or even take advantage of them with their full names" pondered Billy with no intent of actually doing so. He couldn't find his own name which he later discovered was because he didn't fill out a form so got one of the unnamed meals. "Better having a sense of anonymity" he thought as he glanced to see his full name was written in large writing on a patient wristband for all to see so he tore it off.

"You need that wristband, so we don't give you allergies or the wrong pills" said nurse Rachel loudly from inside the glass 'fishbowl' where the fishy nurses rarely swam out of. "I'm pretty sure your system can handle that and use a photo of me for verification" replied Billy to which Rachel quickly retorted "sure, and that system will also record my note that you are being hostile and aggressive."

Totally out of character Billy screamed, grabbed a chair and threw it at no one in particular and then knocked over the meal cart.

"I wasn't aggressive before but happy to be aggressive now if you are going to be a bitch Nurse Ratchet, I mean Rachel" said Billy as other patients or 'consumers', as some prefer to be known, watch on or ignored.

Beeping started again, another 'Code Black' apparently. The beeping reminded Billy of his entry into the hospital. Was it the bomb inside him beeping and would detonate like in the movie *Speed* if he did something wrong? He ran into a room where seven nurses surrounded him and the slightly older patient whose room it was.

Jessie was a self-professed 'feral' with ratty hair and no fixed address since she left home at 16. She wasn't on the streets much, just couch-surfing or in boarding houses usually but didn't like sticking around for long. So she wasn't that bothered when little Billy came in with nurses behind him. He did not have an aura of masculinity like the men she feared.

"It's all good buddy, just chill here, talk it out and they will go away so you can sleep it off with a nap. Otherwise they might inject you or throw you into seclusion" said Jessie softly. "Stay out of it, it's none of your business Jessie!" yelled Rachel to which she calmly replied "He is in my room which you are also trying to enter, this is definitely my business so please shut up!"

Things settled quickly without an injection or seclusion but everything was noted in Billy's and Jessie's records with aggression alerts popping up for anyone who opened the electronic file. Words were also entered like 'overly familiar', 'invasive', and 'entitled' littered around the notes that would later influence the senior psychiatrist (Consultant) and other staff.

Jessie invited Billy to sit on the chair in her room and despite the loud objections of the nurses to get him to leave, they started a conversation. They talked for a few minutes until the shouting of nurses made it too difficult to continue.

Henry later arrived explaining that Billy's mum was too worried about getting Covid to visit but was even more worried that her little boy might get attacked by 'some lunatic'. Both fears were somewhat rational: having asthma made Joy more likely to become very unwell if she got Covid and there were certainly some dangerous and erratic people acutely unwell in that ward.

"So glad to see you Billy, we still love you, it will be OK" said Henry in a way that sounded insincere not because it actually was but because he was uncomfortable expressing certain emotions. Henry was also scared by one patient who looked like an ex-con, he kept pacing and talking loudly to his voices but then said to Henry and Billy "I'm very sorry if I scare you".

Billy was really scared of that patient and really most people because he was the youngest and smallest. It seemed like there were only really concerns and strategies to protect the females which was justifiable, but he also needed some reassurance on safety to help him get to sleep. He didn't believe the stereotypes about people with mental illness always being aggressive and violent but even he had quickly escalated from placid to angry just an hour earlier because that environment and because poor attitudes of staff created anger and violence. Aggression begets aggression and with everyone under the added pressures of the virus, it's a recipe for someone to get seriously hurt.

The TV was also a source of fear and confusion for Billy. News of new infections were reported with irrational people worried to potential lockdown interviewed. This news from the TV was intertwined with the strange thoughts of bombs, cameras and everything flowing into a higher purpose.

"Here's some chocolate to eat and share Billy" but he wasn't concerned for food, "Can you bring my old music player next time please?" he requested, and a nod back was reassuring. Billy didn't realise that as well as his phone locked away, wired headphones needed for his player were banned due to the very small risk of strangulation. There were many rules that were never explained to Billy or were mentioned inconsistently depending on the nurse and a vague guess of likely risks of each type of contraband to each patient. Even sharing the chocolate was highly discouraged but a secret share of chocolate could be like currency for gaining a patient's extra dessert. A generous sharing of chocolate or even the much more forbidden but easy to smuggle in lighter and smoke could ensure that a patient stood up for you to other patients or to nurses acting like bullies.

As Henry got up to leave, Jessie introduced herself to him and promised to watch over young Billy like a big sister. She thought about the right thing to say for a moment and then said: "those of us who go through this crap are like brothers and sisters. It's great to have support from parents like you, mine don't give a shit but what you need to remember is as hard as this is for you, it's a thousand times harder for us." It was the right thing to say for Billy's sake but not so comforting for Henry.

"Dad, Jessie, I don't want to scare you cos I will just panic more and make it worse, but I think they put a bomb inside me" said Billy slowly and incredibly seriously to which his Dad just laughed at. "Sir, please don't laugh at that and Billy, just know that it may feel totally true that things like that happen but you need to question them and think hard about whether they are real" said Jessie from considerable personal experience in a way that brought up some difficult memories of thinking, hearing or seeing strange things in the past.

"You need to be honest to your Doctors about this stuff and let a nurse know if you feel unsafe. They might call you psychotic or say you have something like schizophrenia, but you don't have to accept any labels they throw at you" advised Jessie. "Cos you came in on Friday night, you don't really see your main doctor until Monday after their meetings" explained Jessie.

The weekend seemed to drag on forever with no one prepared to estimate how long Billy might be locked up. Even for

Jessie who had seen many patients come ago from multiple hospitals, the formula for getting a discharge was largely a mystery.

$$\sim 3 \sim$$

THREE

Jessica Sorento grew up in Katoomba -a suburb in the Blue Mountains just outside Sydney. It was idyllic scenery cruelly juxtaposed with family violence in a run-down cottage. Her father used to beat her older brother Sam in front of everyone as a threat to them all. Even when Sam did nothing, their father would punch him in the chest as he walked past. It was worse when Jessie's misbehaviour led her dad to hurt Sam. If Jessie accidently slammed a car door or even gave her dad a certain stare, Sam was the voodoo doll who was harmed to punish Jessie indirectly.

These early experiences were truly terrible and would haunt Jessie for the rest of her life. From the toxic seeds planted by family violence, violence grew in Sam and he cycled the violence to future partners and his children. The same seeds for Jessie though made her fear masculine men and even masculine women.

Most seeds of trauma sprout weeds of hateful violence and fear as had happened for Sam and Jessie respectively. Even so, out of the trauma Jessie also experienced some 'post-traumatic growth' in terms of stronger compassion for others who also went through horrific experiences. The piercing to her heart could have easily made it permanently broken but instead grew an empathetic but resilient 'bleeding heart'.

There was a lot of heroin junkies in the Mountains and Jessie's first boyfriend pressured her to try hard drugs at age 13. She never really became a junkie like the others but was using a lot of ecstasy on the rave and doof scene. She would wear flared paints and beaded bracelets always approaching other party people and making friendships that were intense but transient like many other things in her life.

All the partying took a toll on finances and her mood but helped Jessie figure out how to run awesome events. She took on casual jobs for festivals, concerts and when desperate -corporate gigs. Seeing all the ordinary people in their suits or dresses trying to meet people just to advance their own goals felt totally foreign to Jessie. Many of the corporates came up to the Mountains to escape their mundane city lives or as a retreat in order to be more creative. They brought with them the same mundane mindset and then overindulged on alcohol to assist in their often-regrettable hook ups with colleagues.

Jessie drank occasionally but more often did drugs. Drugs seemed like a way to accelerate Jessie's journey to understanding things beyond the ordinary world. They were instead major diversions to that journey. Jessie experienced super paranoid thoughts after smoking dope. What started as fun missions to explore her neighbourhood and find munchies in the early years of smoking later turned into terrifying suspicion of everyone. It was unpredictable whether each different grade of weed and each number of tokes of a joint or hits of a bong would lead to incoherent speech and misunderstanding what others said or did around her.

The trauma as a kid plus the drugs meant Jessie was more likely to get longer term mental health issues but it is not clear of all the links in that causal chain. The trauma led to connecting with certain type of people which led to being around drugs. The need to get away from bad memories and strong desire to feel connection with new people led to overuse of certain drugs. For those who have had chemicals in their brain like dopamine and serotonin disrupted by their difficult lives, a way of artificially enhancing these chemicals becomes more than tempting.

Still, Jessie knew her limits. Like the tracks around Wentworth Falls, she knew which ones were dodgy and took the risky ones close to the cliffs but turned back whenever things looked exceptionally dangerous. Many of her school friends became addicted to meth very soon after they first tried it. Jessie chose to never even try meth, but the related drugs of speed and ecstasy still took their toll -albeit not as quickly as meth. As the once-innocent faces of her friends became angular and sharp, Jessie avoided being visually marked as a junkie. Still, she carried the stigma of being poor and wearing clothes and jewellery from fringe sub-cultures.

As part of Sydney's small doof scene, Jessie would SMS the party organiser on a Saturday night for the directions to a field where the event was. The music was more fun on acid but after one bad trip on an LSD crystal the size of a single grain of salt called a microdot, Jessie now stayed away from hallucinogens. Instead she swallowed half a pill of ecstasy every hour for six hours. When she had a bad day or just a lot of cash from a corporate gig, she would 'double dump' two pills for a better high. The risk of overdosing or becoming dehydrated and dying were real but ignored.

Somehow the bigger disincentive for taking so many e's than possible death was 'suicide Tuesday'. This was especially a problem when the pills sold as e's had the horse tranquilizer Ketamine in it. Though Ketamine has helped treat pain and in careful doses -also depression, at the levels Jessie was having without realising, Tuesday became a 'k-hole'. The risk of suicide peaked on Tuesday after a big Saturday night session. Jessie called the Child Line and later Life Callback many times and found them very helpful, but one time a helpline operator used caller ID to get the police to come to her house for a welfare check. This is not common practice unless there is a very high risk of suicide and not all organisations will call the police.

Jessie always felt different but had no problem with being a misfit. She knew she was doomed for a difficult life because of her difficult childhood but held out a little packet of hope that she would do something big and purposeful one day. This little packet of hope kept Jessie from taking her life when she was abused, in a depressive hole or just when she felt shit coming down from Saturday night's drug (mis)use.

Jessie had 13 different diagnoses across her many admissions to public hospitals. She enjoyed picking up a new one as she used the fact that they gave her so many labels that contradict or overlap to prove that psychiatry is a pseudoscience. She took her meds when she could afford them and remembered. With so many different pills and injections, she felt like a lab rat being experimented on by a rudimentary medical profession in bed with 'big pharma'.

Meds guided Jessie out of deep holes and brought her back to reality. This occurred gradually when needed but would be faster when partnered with non-medical strategies like long sober and sombre walks in nature.

This admission started two weeks ago, and she would have gone down to the more relaxed 'sub-acute' ward but because of all the homeless people and Covid issues, there were no beds.

Meanwhile, 'very crazy old men' were getting out because if the virus got into the ward, they'd be badly affected.

As some very unwell people were discharged from hospital, those like her got stuck in hospital as 'bed block'. Bed block occurs when there are too many patients and not many being discharged -usually because they have no homes to go to. It is against policy in NSW to discharge a mental health patient to homelessness. There's a loophole in that though and if they refer you to a homelessness service, it's no longer their problem and they chuck you out with a small handful of meds, ongoing illness and a very strong chance that you will come back as 'failed discharge' or new admission in some other ward or hospital. Then you get slowly chewed up and spat out again.

Jessie moved around so much that she knew at least two wards in each of the five hospitals she had been to. The worse wards were usually those called 'high dependency' which were very restricted and tended to have the scariest patients. Jessie would quickly befriend the right people though and not be too quick to leave the warmth, decent beds and tasteless but free food. She would rather sleep rough than in a psych ward but sometimes needed a break from flighting for a place in a shelter, boarding house or spare couch.

With the patchy access to Centrelink that comes with having no fixed address and need to constantly apply for jobs which requires a computer, sometimes Jessie starved for days. Many of her antipsychotic meds slowed down her metabolism and made her hungrier. This combined with her lack of access to cheap and healthy food made losing weight even more difficult. She charted her weight from overweight to a point a dietician in one hospital called 'obese class 3'. "It's harder to ask for food money from strangers when you are a fatty" thought Jessie once.

With so many admissions to hospital, Jessie reached out to social workers as soon as she realised what their role was. They were meant to be there to help her with things like avoiding homelessness and also linking her into services like public housing. With others in the team, social workers can also help apply for funding for more recently established pools of money for people with disabilities from federal government disability funds.

Social Workers during all of Jessie's admission were either absent or adversarial. Absent in terms of just never showing up on the ward or being 'too busy' which the nurses also used as an excuse constantly but at least you saw them on the ward. It took the very assertive efforts of carers to get things happening with social work, but Jessie never really had anyone willing to take full responsibility as a carer. While others got discharged quickly, a friend willing to let Jessie sleep on their couch for a few weeks was sometimes enough to get a discharge and other times seen for what it is: a form of homelessness.

All the time in a ward or wandering around the city not working made Jessie a very reflective person. She pondered many insightfully deep concepts which she often visualised with chalk on the ground. Jessie was adept at explaining ideas that helped others get ahead in life. She had drawn on the ground once a framework of the 'goodness mountain' where you hike up steps from:

1. Do things that feel good
2. Do things for your own good
3. Do things good for others
4. Do things for the greater good

Drugs were clearly making Jessie plateau on step one -the constant pursuit of feeling better and escaping the ordinary. Jessie was not interested in the ordinary. She wanted to be extraordinary. Like the steep hikes around where Jessie grew up, she knew she could climb some even bigger mountains but could also act as companion and tour guide for others charting their own path. Rarely would Jessie do anything except steps one and three. She often looked after the needs of others before her own needs and tried to 'heal the world' with everyday kindness. The kindness never progressed to step four as it was usually seized on by other individuals who didn't 'pay it forward' for the greater good to benefit.

The early life of Jessie and her family was certainly turbulent. She didn't want any more major jolts to her life's course. Still, she wanted her life to flow naturally in exciting directions with unexpected exchanges with random people leading to positive new realisations and mutual benefit for her and for strangers who temporarily enter her life. So, she stopped weed when she realised it was distracting her from her bigger purpose. Other drugs were much harder to avoid.

Ongoing verbal abuse came from partners or drunken acquaintances who owned the couch she was sleeping on and who paid the rent and bills. She never wanted to be a scab or leech so gave whatever money she had and did as many chores as she could muster the energy to complete. Still, she knew when she needed to move on and made many late-night escapes to terminate relationships and start again.

Jessie ended up in Sydney Park one night near culturally edgy Newtown. Under an old chimney stack she met a man who instantly gave her bad vibes. Not trusting her instincts, she bought a green e from him with her last $40 of the week. There must have been hallucinogens like LSD in the pill because after 40 minutes she felt detached from the world like her last bad trip. Paranoia set in. The people around became called 'the jungs' – a new secret race of young people set about on torturing her mentally and physically.

She approached a group of young people sitting on a hill in the vast park. "Did you just call me fat?" Jessie spluttered. One in the group wearing a pink hoodie stood up ready for a fight. "We didn't say anything" said a guy still seated with this repeated by another guy. Jessie was sure they said that and then thought they called her a homeless bitch. She took off her tattered shoes and ran into the dense trees in the park.

That night seemed to go on for weeks. The bird noises from shadows appeared to form into outlines of ghosts on the former kangaroo-hunting grounds of the Gadigal and Wangal clans. This place seemed to be cursed with generations of pain and death now playing out in drug-induced hallucinations.

Jessie woke to the reassuring sounds of children at a nearby playground. She was covered in mud and was thirstier than ever before. She was sweating even more than usual. Her phone was out of credit and almost out of battery, but she knew she needed to talk through what happened last night.

She still had the Mental Health Line 1800 number in her wallet and explained what happened to the operator. The apathetic operator said a crisis team would come out but because it was drug-induced with the hallucinations and delusions only occurring during intoxication, it was unlikely she would be an involuntary ('scheduled') patients forced to stay in hospital. When the crisis team came though, they came with an ambulance and when the team saw the sorry state of her clothes and no shoes, they took her to hospital. When you are brought to a hospital by ambulance in NSW, you are almost always treated as a scheduled patient even if you called the ambulance yourself and went willingly.

If an ambulance comes with the crisis team, it means you are seen as less of a threat to yourself or others but often they come with cops instead or just send cops without any mental health professionals present. This practice is changing slowly with various programs where psych nurses or other mental health professionals go out to relevant calls with the police or ambulance.

For Jessie, she had many confrontations with police called to schedule her and the ambos were mostly only focused on physical health and whether you were suicidal. This time, Jessie was not suicidal and was never homicidal.

She was taken to hospital again and scheduled again but her 2020 admission would be more restrictive and challenging than ever before.

~ 4 ~

FOUR

A week into hospital and everyday was a bit blurry for Billy. He felt cloudy and a fog around him that started to protect him from the bad thoughts. It also made him as slow as the thick drool that built and fell from his mouth to the hospital floor. His thoughts functioned at a snail's pace, but his legs and arms fidgeted quickly with intensely restless agitation.

"It's these pills" Billy told the older doctor. "They're making me nervous... or like I'm covered in slime that tries to slow me down, but my body tries to shake it off." "Sounds like a movement issue which comes with certain medication, we will try another one" remarked Dr Stone as he quickly got up to leave. As they walked out of the consulting room, Billy noticed one of the few cameras in plain sight and wondered "were there also hidden cameras around?"

No one explained what the new cocktail of pills was to Billy, but it quickly became clear that they were not right for him. The search for cameras became intense despite reassurance by patients and nurses that public facilities here are not allowed to install them in patient rooms. Things he was told just confused Billy more. Jokes were misinterpreted with unintended hidden meanings analysed and acted on in unusual ways. A comment about the ward being like Big Brother really resonated for Billy. The idea that people would be stuck in a building in some kind of 'social experiment' seemed like a detail Billy could have missed when he signed the forms entering the building. For everyday people with an interest in becoming reality stars, everyone was very good at acting the part of nurse, doctor or patient.

The Stanford University Prison Experiments showed situations where if you give the roles of prisoner and prison guard to normal people, they quickly assume the roles. Abusive power dynamics formed quickly and with dangerous force in that experiment. A similar situation seemed to be happening to Billy. "I understand what it's like to be crazy now, you can let me out of the experiment" yelled Billy as he bashed on the main exit doors. More pills came but Billy managed to vomit up 1 out of 4 of them a minute later into the nearest toilet.

Maybe they thought he was just a gifted actor with his screaming about the filmed experiment. He seemed to have just showed the other contestants that he was going to be a good ally for the show. He might even be the fan favourite for the first season of whatever show he was in. Four hours of TV a day for your whole life can warp your sense of reality to begin with so the artificial environment of the 'hospital' seemed real to everyone.

The ward was somewhat familiar to those who had grown up with ER, Grey's Anatomy, Scrubs or even the different time and setting of M.A.S.H. which created archetypes of characters now being replicated across the ward. The apparent film set and nurse contestants/actors seemed much more sinister than familiar shows.

Billy didn't understand the 'challenges' of the 'game' he was in. On what grounds would the contestants be evicted? If his screaming before didn't get him out of the game, how else could you 'tap out'? More of a concern was: how were they allowed to give out such strong pills with that confusing form being signed only after entering the building and under a state of daze and duress?

Billy totally believed he was in an elaborate studio and didn't know who an ally and who was an enemy among either other contestants or studio imposters. He decided not to talk too much about the TV show as that might appear strange and expose him as someone who didn't understand the rules of the game at all or how to win.

Seeking out clues on the ward, he realised that there were different levels. Through the window of one door you could see a corridor leading to a similar door with a window. Jessie explained that that was sub-acute as in below the acute level where they were then. Billy knew Jessie was an ally and she started explaining how the ward worked.

There was someone acting very dangerously and walking around in an intimidating way. Jessie called him the 'eagle' -soaring around looking for prey. She talked in a strange code with nicknames in a way that confused Billy so much that he looked for symbolism even in her very direct and clear explanations of life on the ward. Billy's trust in the studio's surveillance waned and he worried that the eagle might attack him. Were there actual crazy people in the show to make it seem more re-alistic?

The worse times were at night. Billy couldn't sleep for half the night and the other half of the night he would have intense nightmares. One repeated nightmare saw him being raped by a female succubus demon who became visible to him for a whole minute in his room after he woke up. He heard moans from other rooms that sounded like they were piped in via speakers to create a spooky atmosphere for the 'up late' episodes of the reality show.

He left his room and saw an older woman acting as the only night nurse. Jessie had called her the owl. She quickly eyed Billy from the nursing fishbowl and swooped in with some more pills which she called 'PRN'. Though 'pills right now' seemed like a better backronym, PRN stands for *pro re nata* meaning 'for the thing born' in Latin. This was a convoluted and pretentious doctor-way of saying pills to take when a problem is born and they are needed right away.

A PRN is a quick fix to a problem but sometimes needed. A problem like nightmares that are so intense that they are sometimes called night terrors will not go away with a PRN. The underlying trauma or other symptoms of distress need talk therapy as well as temporary or ongoing medicine.

The pills could have been just strong herbs that don't need prescription. That would make sense to Billy in terms of how a TV studio could just give them out without much thought. The owl didn't even try to find out the back story to the nightmares, perhaps it didn't make for good television or perhaps she was just a lazy bitch resorting to the easiest solution to shut up an annoying young lad.

"It's OK not to be OK" said the Owl, at least a little bit as wise as her moniker suggested. Was this a sign that Billy should act up a bit more craziness for the cameras or was he indeed very unwell?

The Eagle's room was right near the fishbowl as the troublemakers tended to be moved to either the closest room for observation or the furthest room, so they don't annoy staff so much. With the talking, the Eagle woke up and started screaming about bombs. This made Billy think that the opening scene of his storyline in the show was them pretending to put a bomb inside him. Or was it actually a real bomb and the surveillance was all by terrorists hijacking the hospital?

The Eagle's screams didn't make sense to the Owl, but parts resonated with Billy in unusual ways. Then, as if someone paused filming to go to ad break, the Eagle asked very clearly: "Are you from Wuhan?"

The ward at night was a bit nicer somehow. With no one pacing around, the many fluorescent lights were off with subtle floor lights were on instead. There was less of a feeling of being in a sterile hospital and the corridors were more inviting. Still, many terrible things happened at night with only one or two nurses on-shift to monitor the place. The collective nightmares of trauma often woke one person with their screams acting as a domino effect to others.

Billy had started using a massage chair installed in an alcove of the ward. Though in other hospitals these are locked away in small rooms or not available at all, here a chair could be used to relax and get both a tactile sense but also a deeper proprioceptive sense involving a greater awareness of the body. Billy had a basic understanding of mindfulness and muscle relaxation from Eastern traditions as well as lessons from school which were Western bastardisations of those traditions.

As the massage chair pressed firmly against Billy's neck, he made a long inhale. It continued to massage and then he exhaled for a longer outbreath than his inbreath. Scientifically, this is a way to hack the vagus nerve to ease some anxiety. Billy still felt very tense about being watched and had temporary social phobia has he was fearful of most people on the ward. He tensed his fists with an inhalation then let go of his fists with a longer exhalation and the worries about the virus and thoughts of being on a reality show were briefly postponed.

His eyes closed gently but then he sensed that someone was quickly lunging toward him. It was the Eagle. "Just checking if you were asleep" said the Eagle with a sinister grin. "Next time you do that, you'll become my personal Wing Chun practice dummy on the ward" hoping that the Eagle would not call his bluff under a false assumption that most Asian men know martial arts. The Eagle stepped back and whispered: "I thought we were all brothers in here watching out for each other."

As he shook off that weird interruption he gradually relaxed again as the chair worked his arms and lower body. Billy tried to piece together the jigsaw puzzle that was the last week without ever seeing the whole picture. Maybe each piece was revealed in each episode of the reality show. Maybe it revealed each contestant as a bird which characterised each contestant as a nickname from the fans watching. What bird was he? He wasn't going to be typecast as some Asian bird or even a rainbow lorikeet because people saw him as gay.

He heard laughing from the room next to his. Maybe this guy was like a kookaburra with his laughter being a sign of good luck. He carefully glanced in to see if there was something funny, but the man appeared to just be staring up at the ceiling giggling. Was he a friend or foe in this game?

Alex was a man his forties, very slim and with a very pale complexion. He was constantly checking his door and washing his hands. In a world where most people had started handwashing or sanitising regularly, Alex was now laughing at how sane he now seemed.

Alex noticed Billy and tried to explain the laughing. "I was thinking about all the handwashing that people now do for 20 seconds" said Alex but Billy couldn't see the humour. "I prefer to wash my hands for 18 seconds and have to re-do it if I think about something dirty which usually makes me lose count" he explained. Just the thought of the steps in his compulsive process made Alex jump out of his bed to speed to the shared bathroom with Billy observing.

It was not the actual germs and viruses that Alex wanted to wash off but the contamination of his mind. He had sexual thoughts about Billy from just seeing the exposed and hairless part of Billy's upper chest revealed by his vee-neck tee. Alex was not at all attracted to men but still had intrusive sexual thoughts. This is called sometimes HOCD standing for Homosexual OCD also known as sexual orientation OCD. Alex identified as straight and had never even made out with a guy but constantly doubted his sexual orientation and reminded himself of all the times bullies had called him queer. It might be easier if he were actually gay so he could become out and proud within one of the gayest cities in the world.

Billy sensed some sort of sexual vibe from Alex and wondered whether a cheeky hook-up on the ward could form an interesting sub-plot of the reality show. The set of an asylum wasn't meant to be the next *Love Island,* but Billy felt like some form of intimacy – not full sex, would make him feel better. Without access to his phone, Billy couldn't fantasize about people on his many dating apps. The pills had also made him feel less attracted to those on the ward, but Alex was OK looking, and the Owl seemed to have gone across to the other ward through the interconnected fishbowls.

Billy gave Alex a cheeky look up and down with a very subtle lick of his lips. Poor Alex though just had more thoughts he wanted out of his head and went back to wash his hands another 18 seconds -counting aloud this time. Billy approached closer and gave Alex a nod like it was a question about whether he was up for anything.

Alex's counting re-started and got louder. If everyone on the ward was a bird, Jessie was surely a pelican and she overheard the count and swooped in quickly despite her size. As Jessie directed Billy back to his room, he had a partially formed vision of Jessie as a pelican. This was to become highly fitting for Jessie given medieval symbolism of the mother pelican providing her blood by piercing her chest to sustain her young to save them from starvation.

Jessie had seen some terrible things happen at nights on wards like these. With very few nurses at night and no allied health clinicians on the ward then, the night was dark and full of terrors. Jessie stopped things escalating between Billy and the Eagle and stopped Billy's unintentional triggering of Alex's intrusive sexual thoughts. Both the Kookaburra and Eagle were usually harmless, but Billy still was too unwell to realise how is unusual ideas and statements might be misinterpreted by others with their own issues. The ward was a highly distressed little ecosystem.

The PRN kicked in, Billy fell to his plastic-covered mattress and dreamed about birds gliding over computer code flowing down a river. The pills made the dream less vivid, but it was still there with fast motion of the digital waters headed toward a slowly rising sun.

A few days later was Billy's 21st birthday. He wasn't planning a big night out when he thought about it last year but with the pandemic now officially declared, he would not have been going out even if he weren't stuck in hospital. One nurse noticed his birthdate and bought him an espresso coffee which was a small gesture that he appreciated greatly.

Henry came in bringing egg waffles and egg tarts for his birthday with enough to share to a few nurses or patients he liked. Such small gestures were a nice break from hospital food, routines and restrictions but Billy would also forever remember his 21st as being locked away from his mum, sisters and all his friends except his new friend Jessie.

Billy offered an egg tart to a Scandinavian woman who Jessie called the Osprey. She had only arrived as a tourist a month before and shared with Jessie too many specific details of her recent assault that triggered something terrible in her soon after her 15,000-mile journey from Helsinki to Sydney.

Except for brief interactions between certain patients and small number of intense friendships between people like Billy and Jessie, most patients kept to themselves. There were significant benefits for new people who could learn the rules of the ward by engaging with a helpful peer who had been there more than a week.

~ 5 ~

FIVE

When Jacob came to the ward, he quickly realised that he would be the third and final member of a divine trio with Jessie and Billy. Jacob was from Liverpool in Sydney's South West but taught maths at a school just a few blocks from the hospital where he was now incarcerated.

Jacob ticked Aboriginal on his paperwork when he came in but didn't want any special treatment. Ticking that box was important for him to recognise his nan who recently passed away on country in the Northern Territory (NT). She was one of just 150 people to still speak Ngan'gikurunggurr living along the Daly River near Nauiyu. Her daughter April moved to Sydney as a teenager and married Jacob's father who had British and local Cabrogal heritage.

Though a Ngan'gi and Cabrogal man, Jacob inherited his dad's much whiter skin which came from Jacob's British grandpa. Jacob often 'passed' as a tanned white man without meaning to. His mob around Liverpool didn't instantly recognise him as one of them but then truly recognised him when he explained his connection to country and who was in his deep and vast kinship ties in that area and the NT.

Jacob didn't know a huge amount about dreamtime stories but things like individual totems and clan totems really resonated with him. Crows were particularly important spiritually. The large black crows around Liverpool always confused Jacob as to whether they were signs of good or bad luck depending on their behaviour. Jacob was more settled when he saw a magpie as the black and white pattern of feathers had symbolism of the balance of good and evil like the Yin and Yang that Jacob's Taiwanese wife once explained to him. In some Aboriginal dreaming -the crow represents death. In other dreamtime stories, a bird falls into a bushfire and becomes burnt all over while a magpie falls and only becomes part-burnt preserving some remaining white parts.

One Sunday stroll Jacob walked down Liverpool Plaza. It was desolate due to Covid cases spiking in the area. Jacob noticed two crows eyeing him in flight and then the birds landed right where he planned to walk. A sign of death he thought drawing from some Aboriginal mythology but also felt like he was being dealt two crows or ravens as tarot death cards. Double Death -would he and his wife Cherry get the virus? Was it the spirits of his pop and recently past nan coming to warn him?

He did not say anything to the crows or even think he could communicate with them but still looked for any symbolic gestures they might make. It wasn't clear what this was all about so Jacob just dismissed the thoughts as combinations of coincidence and superstition. To properly dismiss strange thoughts like this, Jacob defaulted to methods of distraction -usually by mentally preparing a lesson plan for the next teaching week.

Jacob had become passionate about the idea of gamification where you bring concepts of video games into real world settings. He already issued students with virtual badges in their online learning system and wondered whether competitive leader boards would be helpful despite the potential to create aggressive competitiveness.

"Life is a game" Jacob exclaimed aloud while picking up the pace of his walk to his favourite café via a riverside park. With no clear transition point, Jacob's imagined what it would be like to be inside a game and then strongly believed he was actually inside a game. Greeting a stranger got 100 experience points (XP). Walking faster meant he might have more time to achieve his mission. Discovering birds and outdoor cats along the way had 50 XP with successful attempts to pat a cat getting 400 XP.

He ran down some stairs and it felt like he had unlocked a new level. Should he explore the map to get new items or try to shortcut to the Mill where his rescue would take place? He jumped past a stack of eight abandoned shopping trolleys looking for enemies that might take away his health points. He ducked under a metal railing, grazed his leg and fell two metres to the park in need of maintenance.

Turning left seemed like an interesting side mission whereas right went to the Mill. He went left, followed the meandering path and encountered two tweens passing a soccer ball to each other. One of the two boys tried to flick up the ball by squeezing it between his two feet but then fell over. "Game Over!" said the other boy which Jacob immediately interpreted as being about him being in a game headed for a dangerous mission.

Jacob then felt the need to ford the Georges River by crossing an overflowing weir. He had crossed the weir before but the rain the night before covered the whole weir so there was a torrent and waterfall down to the lower river. Taking his shoes off to cross, Jacob's bare feet touched the cool rapid flow of the small river and the sensation made him leave the game.

The whole time from the first sense of being in a game to the feeling of the cool Autumn breeze across his now-wet feet,

Jacob questioned what was real and what was constructed by a game or by his mind. He still held some doubt that he was really in a game and wondered whether he just needed a jolt from the real world to end the game-like experience. Just like the thoughts about birds and unusual coincidences like hearing "Game Over!", Jacob only had a feeling that something strange was happening but didn't fully believe his interpretations of the meaning behind it.

Jacob was experiencing what some might label 'breakthrough psychotic symptoms' but they bordered on full psychosis because he acted on false beliefs some call 'delusions'. Jacob didn't think he was hearing voices, but his thoughts were much stronger than before and there started to be distinct sets of voices -male and female and with different attitudes and tones.

Jacob put his shoes and socks back on and walked at a reflectively slow pace to the Mill. There were no interesting new signs of being at the last level of a game at the Mill. He got his regular mocha with no extra sugar and decided to go further along the river path. He walked through a construction area, past some factories that would soon be high rise apartments and into a bike path leading to an old powerhouse converted into an art gallery.

Trying to interpret what had just happened and the sense of being in a hyperreality, Jacob asked the universe for a sign of God's existence and some direction on his purpose in the world. It was a big ask for just a 2.2km (1.4mi) walk along the river to lead to any sort of epiphany but Jacob had faith in country to reveal its wisdom.

He had crossed from the suburb of Liverpool to Casula where three months later a Covid cluster developed. For Jacob then though, the area felt like the Latin meaning of its name –

'hooded cloak'. There were secrets shrouded by thick bushes of weeds. Secrets like the many drownings of children at the river on his left and many deaths on the train tracks on his right.

In the Ngan'gikurunggurr language of his nan comes the word *Dadirri* that roughly translates as 'deep listing'. An Elder from his nan's clan Miriam-Rose Ungunmerr-Baumann explains *Dadirri* as a deep inner spring inside use calling us. Like the River People of his ancestors, Jacob was following the river and deeply listening for meaning in its currents.

At age 25, Jacob already had just over a decade of being recognised as an adult by his clans but he was still in need of growing spiritually and emotionally. His orientation to numbers made him calculate points in his life where he would have kids with Cherry and get a promotion to Head of Mathematics then Deputy Principal and then Principal. These linear structures didn't seem to make sense now to Jacob. Instead, different experiences could be blended and steps to success didn't need such a structured sequence as long as the bigger picture remained.

Jacob realised the time and picked up the pace to reach the nearest train station to get him home faster to shower and go to Cabramatta Yum Cha (Dim Sum) with Cherry. There were no clear signs or symbols along the way and the thoughts of a gamified world retreated. Jacob focused his thoughts instead on how he might explain to Cherry what happened along his usual walk. Having a yarn with his wife was different to sharing stories with his mates because the visual metaphors often confused her. Though her English was very good, specific idioms and cultural references made it sound like Jacob was a bit crazy, so he decided to keep this story to himself for now.

The line for Yum Cha was a bit smaller than usual but still had many people of an Asian background but mostly born in Australia. Almost all were wearing surgical masks which was a lot more common in the 'Little Vietnam' of Sydney's Cabramatta compared with other suburbs nearby but especially compared with the 'Aussie' areas of Sydney. Sydney is a sprawling suburban city with clusters of different cultures and socioeconomic groupings. Like the different dumplings on the trollies grouped together in bamboo steamers, sometimes specific cultures stayed together in one small area of Sydney.

Cherry ordered way too much as usual and Jacob ate more than he should. There was still room for Bubble Tea from one of the 17 boba sellers in a 250m radius across three small blocks. Jacob noticed the tea tasted a bit different than normal. He sensed the temperature and estimated it to what seemed to him to be exactly accurate. He was more conscious of the texture and taste of each boba piece that flowed up the straw than he had ever been.

Intense anxiety about the crowds came from nowhere and paralysed Jacob. Weren't they worried about getting the virus? Would the masks be enough to protect them? A scramble for masks in Cherry's native Taiwan had helped them really 'flatten the curve' despite hosting almost three million mainland Chinese tourists in the 12 months leading up to their first case on January 21.

Jacob started to think about the significance of eating certain totem animals in his culture. Perhaps pangolins or bats had some special spiritual significance with the virus being a form of *Sha Chi* or *Si Chi* but Jacob didn't know enough about *feng shui* to fully form these thoughts. Though the pangolin scales were seen as medicinal in some traditional Chinese medicine, South African tribal understandings of the pangolin or *kwarra* saw them not allowed to be hunted. Bats were clearly linked in Western cultures to death and the taking of life from humans in a vampiric sense. Trying to integrate or reconcile different cultures was always an interest of Jacob but today he was tripping over his diverse thoughts.

It seemed to Jacob that was becoming unbalanced. With school the next day and the prospect of school closures to go to online teaching, the stress of work compounded with Jacob's grief over his nan's death. The rational brain of Jacob's maths education opted for the medical model that he was becoming mentally ill due to stress becoming a catalyst for abnormal combinations of neurochemicals. But Jacob wanted to believe that his feelings were actually some premonition of spiritual unrest.

Jacob did not formally learn about indigenous perspectives of emotional and social wellbeing as alternatives to Western understandings. Still, he had some basic knowledge and firsthand experience of the intense negative impacts possible from any loss of connection to land and water, culture, the spiritual world, extended family, or a community. Jacob had most of these connections intact except for the loss of his nan but felt like there was an invisible cloak covering him and preventing him from fully engaging with the universe or even internally with his own senses.

That Sunday night Jacob tossed and turned so much that he decided to go watch TV. A late-night *Simpsons* re-run was on with an episode where Homer gets messages from her mum using the first letter of each line of a newspaper article. As daylight approached, Jacob started to see things in the shadows of his apartment that were very disturbing. Like ancestral spirits summoned by a Ngangkari healer, the shadow spirits seemed real to him -perhaps unnoticed by the uninitiated.

An alarm woke Jacob from the couch where he had just 90 minutes of sleep. He needed to get ready and drive in an hour to the school where he taught. The public high school was closer to the inner city. The spirits seemed to have went away –perhaps just hypnagogic hallucinations which are fairly normal as you transition from awake to asleep.

In his Volkswagen Polo which he and Cherry call 'Cinnamon', Jacob became very anxious. He switched on breakfast radio to see if the chatter might calm him down. With each lane change and each red light, he felt trapped in his car. The anxiety turned to panic, and each breath became faster but somehow more strained. He felt his heart pulsing through his muscular chest. The thought of being in front of teenagers all day while feeling off made him freak out.

A swerve, a loud horn, a near miss. A quick acceleration, a wrong turn, a scream of profanity.

Everything played out in slow motion and with a feeling like someone else was taking control of the movement of Jacob's hands along the steering wheel and foot on the pedals. He arrived late to school and ran with sweat across his face. No one asked what was wrong -not teachers or students so maybe everything was OK.

Most students at the school seemed ignorant of the risks of the virus and played normally while mostly not wearing a mask. Cherry would have had a fit if she knew how close most students were on the playground and how they rarely washed their hands. Some students started to be more cautious and started sharing their worries about the WHO's declaration of a pandemic a week before. The anxiety of the virus was also contagious.

Jacob randomly decided to change his lesson plan to look at the mathematics of the R_0-the epidemiological principle of how any infections are likely to reproduce from one case. There might be a backlash from senior teachers, or more likely parents for scaring students about the rate in which this Covid might spread but Jacob felt his duty to share this knowledge.

Like his past failed attempts at yarning after too many beers, he put himself as the protagonist in a story of being the first one in the school to be infected with the virus. Rather than the usual interactive style, Jacob attempted a lecture-style format by quickly saying:

"The reproduction number, r-naught, now is about 2.2 with the serial interval about 4 days. Say I got the virus from someone who comes back from overseas, with the virus incubating in my body for 2 days. Now you will see as I draw this negative binomial distribution here and these distribution parameters here, this determines how many people I will potentially infect. For each of those, a serial interval of 4 days can be drawn here which is the average time it takes to infect a new person. If I give the virus to two people before I go into voluntary lockdown, the overall r-naught goes up if we don't have proper testing, lockdown and contact tracing. But perhaps my handshake with Principal Murphy gives her the infection then she is initially asymptomatic. She is infectious but without symptoms she doesn't get tested so infects her whole family who infect others before they self-isolate or go to hospital. Then, the owner of the Principal's local café Sally is missed by contact tracing because the Principal forgot to tell the Contact Tracer and paid cash so didn't have a record. Health authorities only realise Sally could spread the virus after the incubation period when she develops a sore throat and cough which are too late signs to isolate because Sally has already spread the virus to eight of her customers and friends."

The class waited for a pause in the lecture to ask questions while some just wanted the topic changed entirely. Even though they didn't understand everything their teacher had just said, the contagion of anxiety quickly spread across the room.

One student mentioned Jacob's confusing story to Principal Murphy by joking she was a victim of the virus in his story. Petra Murphy was alarmed. Rather than approach him directly, she gossiped about the incident with everyone in the staff room. One of the school counsellors recognised the potential risk posed by Jacob to himself and to his students who started to realise how much the pandemic could spread. Catastrophising by staff and students was a slippery slope to a lot of parent complaints and that would not be good for overall welfare of the school.

Counsellor Graeme suggested that Jacob take the remaining half-day off which Petra and Jacob both agreed to. Jacob also explained that the drive in felt unusual, so Graeme recommended Jacob go to the GP nearby before driving home.

As a new patient and with only a 10-minute slot, Jacob was told he could be very unwell and should go to ED immediately. He drove himself, waited 6 hours to see a junior doctor and was strongly encouraged to admit himself voluntarily to the psychiatric ward. He complied but didn't want this to affect his teaching and generally had a mistrust of large institutions like hospitals because they were complicit in forcible removal of Aboriginal people like him. Though the Stolen Generations were taken as children decades ago, the intergenerational trauma persists.

Jacob realised how this place could destroy his career and got out of his chair in ED. He was disoriented and tried to walk out the ambulance bay, but an alarm went off and someone yelled "he's trying to abscond, put him on a schedule instead".

~ 6 ~

SIX

There were not many activities on the ward despite many being on the adjacent sub-acute ward. It seemed like if you were acutely unwell, boredom was not an issue that anyone was prepared to assist with. There was one Diversional Therapist (DT) who came onto the ward with a game of Jenga. Billy still had unsteady hands from the pills -though not nearly as bad as before. The DT Joe quickly realised Billy was special.

"What do you do mate?" asked Joe. "I do nothing really, just sit at a computer" replied Billy vaguely. "Are you good on a tablet computer?" asked Joe holding a tablet without any cameras. Billy helped Joe fix the WiFi on the one tablet to be shared across the 40 patients in the two wards but only in supervised daytime hours. In exchange, he could use the tablet an extra hour that day. He checked his work email -814 new emails in a week, fuck.

Billy almost completely forgot about the cameras. These thoughts seemed to happen only around dinner but and they were intense at that time. His suspiciousness peaked right when night-time medications were handed out and again before morning meds. Not a coincidence.

Billy noticed himself becoming more creative at certain times of the day but completely devoid of intellect and creativity at other times. These were the troughs when the meds were less strong. At creative times just after dinner and before the tablet was taken to the fishbowl for the night, he would draft code for a new app idea. He decided to make an app to help people with a mental illness.

"What ya typing?" asked pelican Jessie. "It's JavaScript for a mobile website or maybe Android app." "What's it do?" replied Jessie with little understanding of what JavaScript was. "Like a survey but gathers information to learn about someone just enough to recommend someone to talk to before their head gets so fucked up that they end up somewhere shit like here."

"Very cool, how does it sort through so many different problems people have and match them up with someone to talk to?" Jessie asked which Billy quickly answered with a dismissively confusing term of "branching logic". Jessie got it straight away though as she imagined a vast tree with all the possible leaves of treatment solutions growing out of branches and sub-branches of personal problems.

As Jessie drew the tree and Billy tapped away JavaScript as fast as anyone could on a touchscreen, a handsome man is his mid-twenties entered the corridor entering the acute ward.

Two of the Nepalese nurses at the end of their afternoon shift were exceptionally rough with Jacob -possibly because he looked like he might start a fight or bring in contraband. They put on gloves and pat him down which made Jacob immensely uncomfortable. He didn't have anything that he thought was dangerous, but they took his belt, shoelaces, smokes, phone, and even ripped out the string from the hood of his jacket. Then they used a metal detecting wand and took out Jacob's father's metal lighter.

He was given a bunch of forms and sat down to read Schedule 3 which is the statement of rights for detained patients. It was so confusing with the contrast of voluntary versus involuntary and mentally disordered versus mentally ill. Then it mentioned electro convulsive therapy -not the best greeting to be told about the potential to be given shock therapy against your will but it was unlikely luckily.

Jacob approached Billy and asked what his cultural background was given he looked like Han Chinese but dressed like he was Australian born. As Billy's family was from Hong Kong, he spoke a bit of Cantonese which Cherry couldn't understand but both Taiwan and Hong Kong wrote in traditional Chinese. Realising this, Jacob lifted his left sleeve revealing two characters tattooed: ?? and the Latin *veritas* underneath. As well as admiring his biceps, Billy recognised both the characters and the Latin as referring to *truth*.

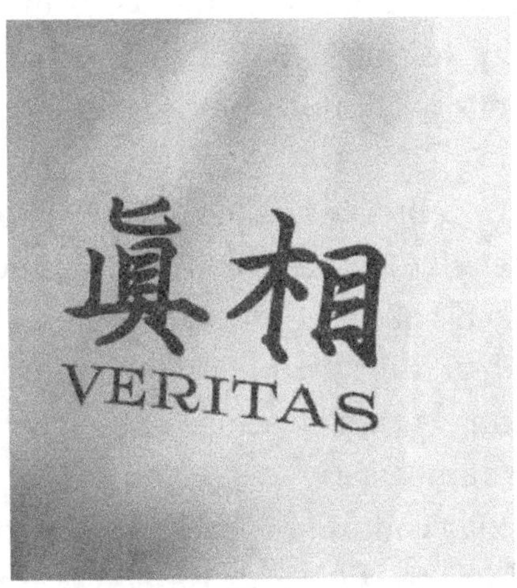

Billy was catching feels for Jacob because of his unique features and nice body. He liked Jacob even more than his looks because Billy loved the idea of the pursuit of truth with *veritas* being the motto for Harvard and displayed on their crimson shield.

Billy quickly developed crushes on guys, girls and a couple of people who didn't identify with any particular gender. It was not a big deal and wouldn't make things awkward, but Billy would definitely make a special effort to get to know Jacob and the meaning behind his tattoo.

Over the next few days, Billy and Jessie learned about Jacob's connection to Taiwan from his wife. Jacob explained his strong interest in truth-telling for indigenous reconciliation. The pursuit of truth was also embodied in Jacob's passion for mathematical proofs which guarantee the truth of a conclusion through beautiful logic.

Jessie's drawing of the intricate tree was thrown out by a nurse and Billy's code turned out buggy when he pasted it from the in-built notes app of the tablet into a debugger online. As the different cocktails of pills starting to kick in at different days and times for Billy, Jessie and Jacob, their shared epiphanies on life and realisations of common past experiences started to occur less often.

Without notice, Billy was asked to move to the sub-acute ward on the other side of the building. It was now totally clear that this was indeed a hospital and not a reality TV studio. Henry visited his son on-and-off with his mum still staying away because of her asthma but also because of the new one visitor per day rule because of the virus.

In sub-acute, Billy could use a treadmill -one of the only ones in a psych ward in the state because elsewhere they are seen as too risky. There were one or two groups per day but mostly these were mundane craft groups which Billy did not have the patience or interest for. He felt like he was back in pre-school which was appropriate given the low cognitive age for one or two patients but insulting to everyone else.

One of the two occasions where he joined art group, he drew crude images of things he wanted to buy when he got discharged but these were dismissed by another patient as materialistic and greedy. The much better drawings of others also angered Billy because he knew if they gave him a digital drawing tablet, he could make exceptional art with such studio quality that it would embarrass those drawing with pencils.

After just a few days on sub-acute, Jacob entered sporting a black eye. A morbidly obese patient they called the Cassowary had punched him unprovoked. Jacob was begrudgingly doing some dot painting after an art therapy student saw he was Aboriginal on his medical records. This had led the aggressive Cassowary to say some disgustingly racist things about Aboriginals after saying he was Hitler-reincarnated. Jacob stood up for a fight and was quickly punched in the face. The nurses did nothing except log the 'incident' and move Jacob to sub-acute.

Billy was delighted to see him and realised how strong their friendship had become so quickly because they were around each other in a small ward and had similar experiences. There were no romantic feelings anymore and only platonic attraction, but Billy and Jacob hugged tightly which led to them both being scolded by nurses under the 'no touching' rule with scowls from some other patients.

Cherry was given special permission to come just after visiting hours given Jacob had been assaulted. She could see how strong Billy and Jacob's friendship had become and was simultaneously jealous and comforted.

"Will the school fire you?" asked Cherry while realising she probably shouldn't ask questions that would worry Jacob so much. "They can't" interjected Billy, "It's discrimination on the basis of psychosocial disability". A Nurse overheard and noted in the electronic records that Billy was 'intrusive with other patients' and 'still elevated' but did not intervene and no one read the note.

Jacob had been watching the news and felt like the shows had been taped just for him. There were obscure references and a string of seemingly related themes that looked as though they were planned to help him formulate a new method of online teaching. This would assist in the learning-from-home that was emerging in other countries due to the pandemic and was now inevitable in Australia. Jacob saw the key as being about ensuring student welfare from a distance.

"How are my Year 9s?" said Jacob to Cherry who wasn't sure but recognised the regret Jacob carried for telling them about epidemiology. Cherry could often see the genuine love and care Jacob had for his students which was coming through now. Even if they hadn't been too badly affected by his mini-lecture, if they found out he was in a psych ward, it would affect how they thought of him and make some fear for their own mental health during lockdown.

Like with many primary school teachers and even market researchers, Jacob used a rating with 5 emoji to identify mood or satisfaction. A score of 1 was a frowning face and 5 super happy. The visual system of rating how things are right now was adapted by Jacob into a set of 9 positive emoji and 9 negative emoji which helped students identify emotions and graph the collective mood of his home class over a term.

Jacob started scribbling these emoji during his conversation with Cherry and sensing that he was distracted still, Cherry got up to leave. They hugged with the uneasy sense of not knowing when Cherry could come back to the ward because of the very restricted visiting hours and fact that the hospital was close to Jacob's school rather than their home in Liverpool.

Billy noticed the confused emoji, the sad emoji and the angry emoji drawn on the back of a spare meal order form. The circle outlines of each emoji intersected like a luxury car logo. Sadness overlapped with confusion and anger in this unintended Venn diagram. Jacob spotted Billy pondering the scribbles and then too noticed how they intersected in an interesting way.

"That's what's wrong with my rating system, the kids can't report multiple emotions at once" Jacob realised and then explained to Billy what he was talking about.

The combination of Billy's coding mindset and Jacob's teaching and maths experience was another serendipitous alignment that seemed to have been brought together by a higher power.

Jacob forgot about the pain of his now swelling eye and become excited about a potential collab with Billy when they both got out of hospital. But the collab was already unfolding in hospital. They worked out ways to interpret self-reported emotions that were entered as checkboxes rather than radio boxes to allow multiple selections. With their own confusing set of overlapping highs and lows, they started to score the severity of each emotion and develop equations to flag more complex issues at an aggregate level and at an individual level.

Unlike the idea encapsulated in the term, 'bipolar', there was not just a sad to happy scale but potential for to identify anomalies like dysphoric mania which overlapped seemingly contradictory emotions at opposite ends of the mood spectrum/pole. Rather than a mood score out of 10 from black at one end to white at the other, there were 8 shades of grey in-between. You could have black mania if you were acting like a 10 but feeling like a 0. The 5 in the middle wasn't seen as baseline normality but rather a potential flag for a feeling of flatness and numbness that needed to be explored further.

All of these numbers flying around seemed to make perfect sense to Billy and Jacob but on reflection later, they both questioned whether something made in a psych ward was just a zany scheme doomed for failure. After much encouragement from one nurse and then threats to take away visiting rights, the guys were forced back to their rooms for bed.

The next day, Jessie was at the breakfast table to the guys' surprise. She had taunted the fat neo-Nazi in order for him to retaliate leading the nurses to move her away from him. Clever in this occasion, but sometimes there are no spare beds with no one able to be moved so stunts like that backfire.

"Ratched said you boys were up late schemin' together" said Jessie referring to a conversation with the passive aggressive nurse who brought her to the ward a bit earlier. Like the three interconnecting circles of Jacob's emoji drawing, Billy could see how Jessie's life experiences could ground the more academic and abstract ideas brainstormed by him and Jacob.

"Maybe you can scheme with us, it could change the world" Billy said with a grin that was half-cheeky confidence and half-jokingly exaggerated. "Draw the tree again Jessie to show Jacob" instructed Billy.

Jessie drew the most beautiful and almost symmetrical tree using an outline on the left side to show the branches and negative space on the right side by shading everything other than the branches. It wasn't the most helpful to the mathematically minded Jacob but he did appreciate the impression of symmetry in the tree outline that was actually created by total asymmetry of internal shading on one side and external shading on the other. It was like the magpie or Yin and Yang again but now clear now the contrast could be directly applied to some sort of wellness-illness divide that was all part of one tree.

The drawing was so intricate that it formed like a vector drawing in Billy's mind that could be turned into a logo or app icon. Later that year with access to his computer and drawing tablet, Billy re-drew Jessie's tree not doing it full justice but still showing off his skills with pride as it rendered into these pixels:

Billy and Jacob were taken-aback with Jessie's design. They felt confident that creations made even in hospital could still inspire and surprise you while challenging assumptions about wellness and illness. Like Yin and Yang in balance, the trio were balancing illness in terms of still not thinking quickly or clearly with the wellness activities involving creativity and social con-nectedness. The hospital had not fostered this wellness in any deliberate way except to over a few lead pencils and scraps of paper as well as a complete lack of most other stimuli. The low stimuli environment breeds severe boredom, but also a nothing-ness that was an unusual asset when this little clique found a shared focus. Jacob heard two voices in his head debating like crow versus magpie and he could see two birds land on the tree drawing.

After breakfast, a 'sensory group' was run by an Occupational Therapist (OT). Billy thought occupational meant the OT Diane could help him get a more fulfilling coding job -perhaps in health or for a charity. The group however was the same stupid mindfulness activity from high school where you get a sultana/raisin, feel its weight, squeeze it slightly to listen to it pop, smell it and then finally chew it slowly and taste it as it bursts. It was an interesting exercise that many people found relaxing, but Billy's thoughts always raced when trying to slow down and focus on mundane things like the wrinkled textures of a dried grape.

Jessie was uninterested in groups unless they involved going out to use the two computers. Finding anywhere half-decent to live would mean she would probably get discharged right away but Covid meant that day leave was prohibited so she couldn't go visit a property. The many landlords she was contacting were not accepting people without at least some brief face-to-face interaction to try to check that the applicant would probably pay rent and wouldn't bring random people to the property who might pose an infection risk to other tenants.

A bigger problem was that Jessie had lost her photo ID that night in Sydney Park. With only the hospital address to send it to, she had to wait at least 2 weeks for it to arrive in order to even be able to sign a temporary lease. There were other options like boarding houses and the HomeLink homelessness service, but she had used up all her government-allocated nights for temporary accommodation.

It is the policy of the Health Department running all the public psych wards across the state to not discharge a patient to homelessness unless there is a referral to a homelessness service. This meant one of two things for patients like Jessie: being flicked to three nights' accommodation if HomeLink had spots when you called each day or becoming stuck in hospital long term while you wait for other options. Jessie had already consumed the maximum of 28 days within the last 12 months and even the exceptional circumstances of the Covid lockdown were apparently not enough to override the limit. It was bureaucratic nonsense while homeless people near the city centre were about to be given temporary access to over 300 hotel rooms for free because of Covid.

Jessie looked at her tree drawing and imagined a treehouse to live in with birds visiting each morning as her only alarm clock.

~ 7 ~

SEVEN

The trio had a clear goal to get discharged right away -as was the goal of all patients except one or two who had lost hope of finding somewhere safe to live with enough supports for their needs. For the trio, it was an individual goal but also a goal they had for each other with each of them looking for ways to manage the impressions of the clinical staff and hint at signs of progress in the wellness of the others.

Some may call this 'impression management' while most nurses labelled it 'manipulative' but it was really about doing whatever they could to get their needs met within a rigid institution governed by archaic legislation. The NSW *Mental Health Act 2007* was amended in 2015 to have much more of a focus on consumer rights and helping with recovery in a less restrictive way but this is difficult to enforce.

Even in the five years of the more positively oriented amended Act, Jessie found it unnecessarily coercive and punitive. Her discharges from wards were not properly planned and she did not have any guidance on what to do after an admission in order to prevent a future one. She was stuck inside the revolving door of the health superstructure. At least it wasn't the revolving door of the corrective system with many of her friends and ex-boyfriends in-and-out of jail, but it still felt like an incarceration as it is when admitted on a schedule (involuntary).

Even though they'd only been in the system for a week or two, without leave due to Covid-restrictions and few visitors, Billy and Jacob felt imprisoned with no discharge date even discussed. Prisoners have a sentence and can assume a likely parole date, but subjective psychiatric pseudoscience and availability of accommodation seemed to be the only things governing whether the goal to leave hospital would be achieved anytime soon. There was the opportunity to plead for discharge to an Inquiry and later a Tribunal, but the power is largely in the hands in the treating team who give most of the information in the hearing.

In what feels like court for committing a crime, those who are meant to be paid to help you recover and leave hospital usually fight the case against this goal. Their goal is meant to be to have you in the least restrictive environment suitable for your care needs but usually the only options are highly restrictive hospital settings and almost totally unsupported returns home. Getting carers on board with enough knowledge on your care needs or setting up wraparound services to help prevent a relapse takes time and often fails.

For Jacob and Billy, their fairly supportive and understanding carers and stable homes meant they might get out much faster than Jessie but potentially too fast for their own good.

Every second Tuesday was scheduled as the Inquiry or Tribunal sitting day -done remotely due to the virus but also because such a practice was well-established. Jacob and Billy coincidently had hearings one after the other with the same incompetent sweaty old fat man from Legal Aid. Jacob had called the Aboriginal Legal Service, but they said they didn't support issues to do with the *Mental Health Act.* Luckily, Cherry was a paralegal and had done some research on this Act and explained key parts of it clearly and quickly to her husband.

Jacob got 6 minutes with the lawyer which was not enough to properly explain that if an order was given, it would probably be for three months, but discharge could still be authorised by a doctor.

Entering the tribunal room was intimidating and there was only one person at the Inquiry rather than the three other patients talked about with tribunals. Cherry was there too as support but was not confident to assert aspects of this area of law as she was only a paralegal and not working in health law.

"Do you know why you are in hospital?" asked a man in a suit via video link. "I had some thoughts about birds and computer games then said some things I shouldn't have about the virus spreading, then..." the Legal Aid lawyer gave a subtle shake of his head to suggest that Jacob not go too far down those rabbit holes. Cherry knew there was nothing from a legal or carer perspective she could say to fix this now. A string of confusing questions and clarifications on doctor's notes quickly followed and without much internal deliberation, a 3-month Involuntary Patient Order (IPO) was handed down.

All these medico-legal terms were lost on Jacob even with his university education. The ongoing symptoms and drowsiness for medications made it hard to figure out how to best defend himself without becoming angry and getting defensive about what he knew to be basic human rights. "Fuck!" he yelled which unintentionally scared Billy who was in the adjoining room ready for his 6 minutes with the underpaid and underprepared lawyer.

Billy wanted an expensive private barrister instead of this guy but couldn't afford it. He was also told that Legal Aid have more experience with these inquiries so can usually get better outcomes than private lawyers, but Billy wasn't so sure. With just 6 minutes, no one could get enough information to properly defend Billy and explain how all the unusual thoughts had now gone away. The lawyer could quickly tell that Billy was fully present in the small consulting room and readied his new client to self-advocate for immediate discharge.

Henry was there to support his son but wasn't sure what to say so kept quiet. Dr Stone submitted a detailed report of the last two weeks of Billy's reserved but open admissions of delusions which the Legal Aid lawyer had skimmed and noticed a clear progression from illness to some form of wellness. In Dr Stone's absence, the Registrar Dr Bina gave a forceful but rookie defence of the need for ongoing involuntary treatment. The IPO was denied, Billy could leave the hospital within two hours.

With the rush to get his discharge medication and gather his belongings Billy barely had time to say goodbye to his brother- and sister-in-arms. It was under three weeks that he'd known Jessie and Jacob, but they were already a family by choice -by spirit even though not by blood. He gave Jacob a low-contact hug with a pat on the back but Jessie a bear hug with a reassuring squeeze.

Henry became increasingly worried as Billy left with only a few belongings in clear plastic garbage bags. The tracksuit pants Henry had bought Billy a few nights in were falling down because the drawstring was removed by nurses and could not be easily put back in now.

Billy woke up the next day -April 1. He was excited but cautious of his annual April Fool's Day prank from his Eldest sister but she had moved and felt awkward that she had not visited Billy or even called while he was in hospital. With at least another week of work though, Billy's mum Joy got him out of bed for a walk around the bay to help him unpack the 19 nights in hospital.

Under three weeks didn't sound like a long time but the average stay is just 9 nights. There are pressures nationally to keep this average down to save money and not let patients become dependent on the system. Still, Billy found it hard to explain to his mum all the unusual thoughts, strange people and intense connections made with Jacob and Jessie. He decided to gloss over most things but the reflection on the dark waters of the bay made him reflect on how the flow of his life and been completed diverted and might now stagnate.

Billy stopped and messaged Jacob to clarify something on rivers and birds that made sense in hospital but now seemed strange and obscure. Jacob would not get the message until he was given a few minutes to check his phone later that day. The thoughts in Jacob's head were becoming more like external voices and one sounded like an old friend. Later Jacob replied to Billy simply with a name and a phone number of his old friend.

The name sounded Tongan or something but turned out to be Maori. Aroha was half-Maori and half-Indigenous and liked to joke that he was a Double First Nations person. His name was similar in connotations with *aloha* in Hawaiian which made Billy think someone with a thick Chinese accent was trying to say *aloha* -just a little bit racist. In Maori *aroha* means empathy and compassion. Aroha was perhaps only in his early thirties but full of wisdom.

Aroha met Billy and deeply listened to Billy's stories then realised the extent of the healing process Billy still needed to go through. Talk of myths and nature would only confuse Billy so Aroha mainly listened and pointed out natural things in the built environment that surprised Billy and made him more mindful of urban ecology.

Aroha and Billy met for the second time in Parramatta – 'the place where eels lie down' in the local language of the Burramatta. Billy was now more mindful of entering the lands of different clans and tried to find out which land he was on. As well as checking tribal maps that were previously fluid and disputed, he checked the maps of the local health districts with the constant worry that if he flipped out again, he might end up in some hospital worse than before.

The worries about rehospitalisation might become self-fulfilling prophecies. Though it is good to have an emergency management plan and steps to take in crisis depending on where you are and what time it is, all the different hospitals and opening times of helplines made everything so confusing and hard to plan for.

Billy crossed a footbridge over the Parramatta river -only a small drop to the water but it made him obsess over his own mortality. Such an existential crisis wasn't new to Billy, but he felt closer to death than ever before even with no thoughts of suicide. Aroha reminded him of meditative strategies to chill out focusing on 5 things he could see, 4 things he could hear, 3 things he could touch, 2 things he could smell and 1 thing he could taste. It wasn't enough.

He tried a skill called TIPP where T is for tip the temperature by holding something cold like ice or touching a metal railing to your wrist. I is for intense exercise which Billy did with push-ups and then running on the spot. He looked a bit odd, but it seemed to be working. P is paced breathing with a long inbreath, but even longer outbreath repeated several times. The extra P was for progressive muscle relaxation like in the massage chair but done by himself tensing and releasing each major muscle group while breathing deeply and being mindful of the difference between tension and relaxation.

He knew these skills and he knew they worked but without Aroha there to remind and reassure, he would've had a total mental block accelerating the crisis to breaking point.

Aroha pointed up to Old Government House and started a story about colonisation to distract Billy from others. The pain of Aroha's First Nations ancestors hurt Billy more though. He had thought about the odd racist Anti-Asian remark and how it affected him. As well as racism, he thought about the generations of gay men who were bashed and murdered but had not thought much about how intergenerational trauma might be passed down for Aboriginal and Maori people. There were also still elements of neo-colonialism repressing and replicating problems like the gap of health inequality. There was a massive overrepresentation of LGBTQI+ people in the mental health system and similar inequal figures are reported for indigenous people.

Though Australia is tolerant and progressive on many fronts, these health gaps still exist as wicked problems. Maybe Billy's coding skills could help bridge information gaps and make services better known and more accessible to those who need them most.

Billy started to think about Jessie and all the pain she went through even just in the small snippets of her life story she shared. He thought of Cherry and Jacob and how this episode me that have completely derailed their plans for a 'happy ever after' -even more tragic than the derailment of his own life.

The pain of his friends and those in the hospital started to penetrate Billy's mind. He was more fragile and exposed to these events than ever before but luckily had a strong empathetic new mate there just listening and reassuring. Aroha already had two young sons and was fatherly to Billy without being paternalistic or overly masculine. Aroha had always been told to 'harden the

fuck up' which was still tempting to say now given Billy's soft-
ness, but a gentle and nonjudgmental approach was all that was
needed here. Aroha would not hesitate in calling an ambulance
if it was needed but there was no immediate danger to anyone
here and it just took patience and listening to verbal and non-
verbal signs of coming back from the edge of crisis.

"We are brothers Billy" said Aroha slowly. "Brothers are
bound together for life and remain brothers even if they fight.
We haven't been through the same shit but we have both been
through some terrible times and now I'm here with you to watch
you bring yourself out of these times" reassured the new friend.
Billy had already learned a lot from Jessie's sharing of her experiences and ways of coping but because Aroha was further along
in his recovery journey and better at sharing the right story at
the right time, he was seen by Billy to be a better role model for
now. Still, Billy had learned a great deal from Jessie and Jacob
which would help him in his recovery and could be encapsulated
somehow in the app.

On the way out of the park Aroha acknowledged the symbolism of moving off the bridge despite paralysing anxiety and
panic and Billy was genuinely congratulated. They spoke about
all the annual events in the park but wouldn't happen this year
because of the virus. They were all cancelled for the year but
perhaps you could see them as postponed until a time when they
will be even more appreciated.

Billy remembered that today was the Qingming Festival
which he didn't really observe himself but knew he should be
with his family. Aroha shared a similar degree of respect for ancestors as many Chinese people albeit with very different rituals
and meanings.

The tombs of Billy's ancestors would we swept in Hong Kong
that day by his Aunty and cousins. Henry and Joy would rem-

inisce about their parents and grandparents and burn fake money as symbolic offerings albeit without any special religious significance for them. Both of Billy's sisters would come home that Saturday night for many of their favourite dishes and eat favourite snacks of their ancestors.

Highly elaborate miniature paper versions of luxury goods were burned on that day to try to create good fortunes for ancestors passed. In his home in Sydney, a brass bowl burned the fake money and into it Billy placed his work ID with the intent of grieving his life before hospital with the innocent smile on his photo melting in the small flames.

The experience with police, the hospitalisation, conversations with Jessie, Jacob and then Aroha, the ideas and actions were flowing from a slowly meandering river. There was a temporary stagnation but now everything was ready to overflow into rapids gushing in an exciting new direction.

~ 8 ~

EIGHT

As Billy started to see his new private psychiatrist Dr Lowenstein by video conference, he asked about a diagnosis. The discharge summary the hospital gave him said just 'mental condition' as one diagnosis and 'acute and transient psychosis' dated later on. Billy didn't like the term psychosis -he wasn't sure if 'psycho' was better than being labelled schizophrenic or 'schizo'.

Like many LGBTQI+ people and African Americans, people diagnosed with a disorder have been labelled with terrible terms, but some have reclaimed them. Billy called himself a fag once even though he had been with girls, it felt like he was taking the power away from every bully who had used that word against him. The gay guy he was with when he used this hateful word angrily disagreed and was offended by Billy's use of it.

What mattered was not really the diagnosis but more the symptoms right then as well as the set of symptoms most likely to occur next. AI in an app might work to profile symptoms and experiences as well as gather demographic info like indigeneity and sexual orientation to advise on self-soothing strategies. It could also determine the best places to find the right person to talk to depending on location and time of day. This would require next level coding, with good tech and a team to work on it -not something Billy could do himself.

Billy was starting to become more confident in his ability to promote his ideas to get others on board. Jacob could help with incentivising progression through the app like it was a serious game and also help with ways to simplify all the bullshit medical and legal terms employed by elitist lawyers and doctors.

If he hadn't completely burned the bridge with work like he had burned his work ID, he could get a server rack to power the app as part the company's corporate social responsibility efforts. His friend knew some young billionaire IT entrepreneurs who might throw in some capital as a social venture where you charge for some services but this income feeds back into programs with a social benefit.

Should he just focus on getting better? Billy reasoned that doing purposeful things like using your existing skills and networks to help others might be helpful to recovery. This would only be the case for as long as he managed his stress and was realistic with deadlines. He was not interested in being a sole Founder or eventual CEO, but the idea of CTO and Co-Founder appealed to him greatly.

Billy worked away planning and coding a new app he codenamed with the working title of the 'Tree of Well'. For almost two months while working on the app there was no word from Jacob or Jessie. Billy called the ward, but they recognised it was him as no one else asked for Jessie and only Cherry and Jacob's mum called him. The nurses would not let him speak to them and would not say whether either or both of them were still there. That still didn't explain why they didn't answer their texts.

It had turned out that Dr Stone lectured Jacob and Jessie about the need to not be friends with any patients after a discharge. He saw too many potential risks from keeping up a friendship with someone you met on a ward like being exploited or going through too many of your own recovery challenges to be in a position to help others. Dr Stone explained that Billy was particularly susceptible to vicarious trauma which is trauma experienced from hearing about or witnessing someone else's trauma. He used the metaphor of a membrane that was growing stronger but still semi-permeable so outside influences could come in and weaken the overall structure. Jacob appreciated the scientific reference but Jessie only half-understood even with her talent for understanding complex ideas when expressed visually like this.

Billy asked his new psychiatrist why his friends were not contacting him. "Sometimes patients in hospital become embarrassed about how they acted there and are worried about staying in contact with people who know very personal things about them" said the doctor who had just started his practice after a decade working in a public psych ward. Billy did not accept that explanation as that didn't seem to fit with the kinds of people, he knew Jessie and Jacob to be.

Video conference-based therapy was almost a necessity during the lockdown and the federal government started to put millions into teletherapy, telepsychiatry, mental health research, suicide prevention and digital mental health. Assumptions about lockdown leading to greater domestic violence and suicide were true for many and later evidence showed other serious issues. As the year progressed it was discovered that Covid may have been increasing cases of psychosis on two fronts:

1. Fear of Covid infection, financial burden from job losses, and social isolation from lockdown triggered psychosis for a small sample.
2. Inflammation caused by symptoms of Covid infections led to psychotic symptoms like hearing voices that aren't there (auditory hallucinations) in another sample.

People impacted both indirectly and directly by the virus seemed to be at higher risk of psychosis. Billy acknowledged the studies as small and overly academic but incorporated some more variables into his app's branching logic to look at possible stressors and triggers. More interesting than the scientific studies, Billy found news stories about a sharp increase of people in their 50s and 60s developing psychotic symptoms in China during each surge in the virus.

Like Billy's paranoia about cameras, he could see how a thought about becoming infected could trigger less rational thoughts about every possible way you might catch the virus and then die painfully from it. It was just an assumption about the experience of others but even the research that had emerged from reputable scientists and news sources, showed only a very early and basic understanding of the indirect impacts of a pandemic of this scale.

The beauty of Billy's app idea is that if it got enough users would be to also be a source of real-time research on current symptoms and effectiveness of particular helplines, websites or other apps in terms of whether the user comes back to the app for different resources. This was next level business intelligence stuff on top of the AI branching system and could get research money as well as money as a digital mental health tool. It could support and refer to what already existed in the sector or identify niches for new social enterprises or existing agencies and charities to fill.

Billy soon hit a wall. His back was sore, his eyes red and he was skipping meals to get things done. Time to test some of the principles in the alpha version of the app. The stress reduction and time management strategies appeared to be what he needed, and Billy took four days' break to regroup and reflect.

Maybe Billy didn't have the networks to get the right people working on his idea or the skills to do it himself. The new pills were again giving Billy the shakes all the time and making him feel constantly tired. They were still worth these side effects because they kept him out of hospital and stopped most of the paranoia. An underlying anxiety and a sense pain over the pain of others still distracted Billy from his goals and he could rarely ensure both a focus on the app and basic self-care like walking, meditating and even showering. One self-care aspect that was no longer a problem was sleep but this went from being a healthy 8 hours to a debilitating 17 hours. In the remaining 7 hours of the day there wasn't much time to work on the app.

He felt like he was on some kind of perverse rollercoaster. The highs were leading into hospital and continuing during interactions with Jessie and Jacob despite the sedating pills. There also seemed to be an upside-down part to the roller coaster with strange thoughts becoming disorienting with some strangely fun moments but mostly fear. Now though, were long and gradual lows, lower than Billy thought possible like the rollercoaster and entered a subterranean dip with no one seeing how far down it was going except him.

Work started leaving messages for Billy while he was sleeping, and he finally found enough energy to return a call. Was he OK? When might he be back? Would he send a report detailing his fitness to return to work? "I've been in an asylum, I'm never going to be fit for work again" he said regrettably as it was of course wrong and he could happily return when he got the deep depression and other symptoms back in-check. His manager Steve had suspected that with the non-specific communications of Henry, Billy may have indeed been in a psych ward but really didn't want to know specifics and just wanted any form of green light from a doctor.

"I hate to remind you, but you have a notice period of 6 months" said Steve. Billy then remembered agreeing to this unusually long potential wait from resignation to a final day. Without a uni degree Billy thought he might have to agree to clauses like this to still earn decent money. He would need to resign immediately then get doctor's certificates for the full 6 months but how could he legally or maybe just ethically start a new project or new job still employed and on a non-compete clause. The app wasn't a competing company but could still be claimed as intellectual property owned by his employer.

Not thinking clearly, Billy started scheming ways to get fired! Thought experiments played out as scenarios that both amused and shocked Billy in terms of how elaborate they needed to become. The ridiculousness of this process made Billy reconsider going back to work and he went to his doctor to see if he was ready to return.

Dr Stone's report clearly stated that Billy should have another two months off as he was still susceptible to stress-induced relapse of psychosis. Having only seen Billy after his hospital admission, the private psychiatrist Dr Lowenstein reported that Billy would be likely to work well three-days per week as it would give him purpose and structure. Steve had to liaise with Human Resources about the return to work plan based on the contradictory reports and sent Billy to another doctor which retraumatised him again by having to recount the worst details of 2020 so far.

The third psychiatrist who wrote the report on fitness for work was so used to writing reports to deny workers' compensations claims that he totally downplayed the risks work posed to Billy's mental wellness. Unlike Dr Lowenstein who saw work as a protective factor, this ruthless new doctor just saw Billy as lazy with the goal of leaching off his parents now that his paid sick leave had long run out. This was unfairly inaccurate.

Billy left the doctor's office in the city centre where a small cohort of workers were starting to come back from months of remote working from home. Billy didn't know what he wanted to do with his time now but decided if he was going back to the office, he needed to reinvent his style and approach to work. He bought some white linen button-ups, black jeans, plain white tees and a black leather bracelet. The quick shop made him feel like he was recrafting his identity and making a statement back at work that he was more a mature and interesting person.

Fortunately for Billy, his leave from work was not as well noticed as it would have been in a normal year. For those who knew him but were outside his immediate team, they assumed he had reduced his hours and was not coming to video conferences outside of his team. A contractor had taken over Billy's coding efforts and was asked to cut to two days so Billy could work his preferred three days back in their Pyrmont office.

The many cameras around the casino did not bother Billy as he walked to the nearby offices but his bad experiences with intimidating hospital security meant he didn't want to go into the hospital via security at the doors. It was a by-product of heavy-handed approaches in wards that should act less like prisons and more like hospitals.

In lunch breaks, Billy grabbed some free snacks from the kitchen then a sandwich or fish and chips on Fridays to eat by the wharf. With just a few seagulls around and a few joggers, Billy looked across the water to the new casino that was nearly finished construction. Billy remembered drawing this tower in a ward art group with criticism by others for his crude etching and his greedy goal of one day owning one of the four $40 million apartments. At least he wasn't aiming for the even more expensive penthouse the casino owner would probably take for himself using dirty money of his casino empire with portions allegedly derived from gamblers who were war criminals, money launderers, terrorists, people traffickers and child sex offenders.

Fighting gambling in the inner city became a new objective for Billy's temporarily shelved app. He also acknowledged the true centre of the state's poker machine losses -where Jacob lived in Liverpool-Fairfield. The app would need to react to a diverse set of problems and figure out the links between them to get the right help before they happened or quickly after they first might be recognised.

After lunch, a virtual town hall was convened by one of the billionaire co-founders of the company who was in his early 40s. It was a post-quarantine re-group including reflections on anxiety and stress of Q2 2020 and plans for half the company to alternate when they came to work in Q3 as Team Blue or Team Greem. Billy was a bit insulted by the hyperbole used to describe what obviously were tough times for everyone but nothing near as intense as the experiences of those locked in psych wards with no leave or those in prisons with no visitors.

'We are building a 180m global headquarters which is a steel tower with an internal wooden skeleton and a spiral of terraces on each floor with trees and gardens'. It was a poetic contrast to the 270m high casino, hotel and apartment tower at the other end of the inner city. The brief opportunity to ask questions was seized by Billy and he asked if spaces could host social ventures as new partners to the company -perhaps green tech to suit the green spaces or mental health apps used by the employees in their new wellness pods.

Billy was surprised to get a response and more surprised of its detailed optimism for the idea. The co-founder had already thought of a similar idea when planning how to ensure space was utilised if Blue and Green teams still alternated when the building was ready if the virus was ongoing or if working from home formed into a continued norm.

Billy was fortunate to work for such a forward-thinking and socially conscious company even if they were still laser-beam focused on profitability. He could also capitalise on cancel-culture to avoid missing so many things that were meant to happen while on leave.

Being without leave in 2020 was dangerously restrictive but at least his admission was short, and he didn't miss much while the world was locking

~ 9 ~

NINE

As his students were approaching winter holidays, Jacob was in hospital for over three months. He had gone from smoking half a pack of smokes a day to not being able to smoke at all because leave was still cancelled. He grabbed two smokes and a lighter from Cherry's purse one day despite her becoming worried about being blamed for it. That night straight after a check by the nurse on duty he went to one of the shared bathrooms and turned the shower to try to mask the smell of the smoke which he blew into the trickling water to make it dissipate slightly.

It was a big risk of setting the smoke alarm off and forcing an evacuation which was very difficult on a locked ward. A minute later a nurse came past and noticed the hint of smoke so quickly entered the bathroom with her key. After screaming and swearing inappropriately, the nurse grabbed the smoke from his mount and lighter from the sink.

They couldn't cancel Jacob's leave like pre-Covid procedures so decided to ban all his visitors from the ward for two weeks. "Fuck you Ratched, that can't be bloody legal. We're already locked up for months and you're now punishing me and my wife." He knew the risks a fire could have on the ward and potential for arson by patients using lighters but the nicotine gum they gave out was just not the same and he was becoming more agitated each day with a feeling he was suffocating in the ward.

He threatened to sue the hospital and the nurse personally for false imprisonment. The restrictive powers of the Act never foresaw this level of restriction from a pandemic and only became more restrictive with amendments that year bestowing new powers across a huge suite of different legislation.

Someone could get extremely hurt as contagions of agitation, aggression, and a feeling of unfair total lockdowns might lead to a scuffle turning bad and causing a major injury or death. Jacob would not perpetrate physical assault, but his current mix of emotions could have unpredictable consequences triggering more aggressive patients to act out. There were many new patients coming and leaving the ward -most harmless but one or two had a short fuse and criminal record. Those with a violent past were only placid through sedating medication and because most people stayed away from them.

One patient Jessie called secretly the Ibis because she removed food from bins like these birds known in Sydney as bin chickens. She was a scavenger for food but also seemed to feed off the misery of others often squawking with laughter when someone was crying. Her laughter was frequent and usually random with it turning out she was responding to funny things voices in her head said about other people or when they recounted funny stories from her actual or made up past. The Ibis was also a smoker and after hearing about Jacob's attempt at smoking, she asked him for a smoke and he gave her his only one left - hidden so well that it wasn't discovered during the comprehensive search after he got caught. The Ibis held on to it along with her own matches until one rainy day where she went to the courtyard to light up under her hood.

One camera was pointed across the courtyard, but it was not monitored, and its recordings were rarely used. It was really there as a deterrent for things like smoking but that didn't usually work if someone smuggled in smokes and lighters desperate for as many draws of the cigarette as possible before someone noticed.

As the Ibis didn't have any visitors, she could see any consequences bit the nurses had a creative talent of inventing them even when everything seems like it has been taken away. She finished the smoke with no one noticing and sat laughing in the rain. When someone finally came past to bring her in from the rain her clothes were soaking wet to the point of being very noticeably heavy. The younger assistant nurse was sympathetic as she was also a smoker but handed over the incident to the other nurses who increased how frequently the Ibis must be observed and made her watch as they punished Jacob with an extra two weeks without visitors.

Though it was true, the nurses just assumed that the cigarette came from Jacob and there are no assumptions of innocence or fair use of evidence to justify a punishment. Jacob wrote down three of the highly stressed and rude nurses names to a piece of paper in his wallet titled 'Target List'.

Over that four weeks of adding no visitors to no leave, Cherry was allowed to see Jacob once and only for two minutes to pass on winter clothes. She gave him a hug and was clearly angry with him and the hospital for cancelling her right to see her husband. Even Jacob's oversized hoodie didn't fit any more. He had gained 21kgs in hospital despite the efforts of the competent dietician and his one hour a day on the treadmill. It was the pills.

Jacob had thought about hiding pills in the back of his mouth to spit into the toilet later. He could clearly see the benefit of the different pills working together on mood, anxiety and stopping the strange thoughts but at what cost? The growing belly and disappearance of his chiselled face didn't worry him in terms of how he now saw himself but more because it would affect how others see him and what they might speculate happened to him.

No cards, flowers or chocolates came for Jacob and these were very rare for anyone to get. He wasn't bothered with gifts but the sentiment behind them would be nice. Telling everyone he was in hospital for some physical health issue might be a difficult white lie to keep because if that was the case, his friends and colleagues would have been told and some would have indeed sent things or even visited. He had been injured mentally but these are treated very differently than physical injuries or diseases.

Jacob went out into the courtyard and bounced a basketball in need of more inflation. The stand for the basketball hoop had fallen over again on the uneven ground -luckily not injuring anyone or shattering the backboard. A magpie flew in to perch on the high fence. It reminded him of Billy and perhaps was going to inspire Jacob's next tattoo.

Noticing the mostly black but bits of white patterning of the magpie's feathers, Jacob pictured his future son as mostly Chinese-looking due to the more dominant traits but still with hints of Jacob's own mix of Anglo and Aboriginal features. Would he also inherit what Jacob's doctors were now calling schizophrenia? The fear of this label for himself was one thing but it was much more terrifying to think that he might pass done 'defective schizo genes' to his kids.

Talking to Dr Stone about his deep concern, the risk of getting schizophrenia turned out to be six times the normal population for people with first degree relatives like parents who had it. Though still a low chance, Jacob was not a gambling man and used this conversation with the doctor as a way to request a family meeting with Cherry so he could see her despite the visiting restriction to explain the risks for their future family.

Cherry assumed that the family meeting meant Dr Stone might be considering letting her husband out soon. This was normally a safe assumption as planning occurred with families or carers to check there are supports out of hospital. When she saw her husband's face though, she knew something was wrong.

Completely undiplomatically after a quick hug Jacob said to Cherry "if we have kids, they might get schizophrenia too". Cherry was not completely surprised as her parents back home had suggested the same problem but like any hereditary trait -the odds were not guaranteed and there was no reason to not have your own children just to avoid one unlikely scenario. "The odds are only 4% but there is trauma or drug use that we can't stop, the probability doubles" said Jacob which Dr Stone did not correct. The numbers weren't exactly right but having numerical values always helped Jacob make decisions and he wasn't one to take risks.

The intermittently present voices now become very loud like they were both inside and outside Jacob's head:

"Leave her, you will make her kids pscyho"

"You will be a burden on everyone, just cut all your ties and start again"

"Turn to God, He will protect you and Cherry, and the odds will fall in your favour"

"Don't tell them anything, they will lock you up forever"

"Nan would be ashamed of you *bunji*"

Cherry and Dr Stone were speaking to him, but Jacob couldn't concentrate because even the voices in his head were talking over each other to compete for attention. He stormed out and, on the way, lied about what was going on by saying he had a headache. He then asked a nurse for a strong benzo which he was allowed occasionally as it was charted for him as a PRN. It was not enough to fully settle him but even the sensation of swallowing it settled him slightly.

Jacob looked for something to distract him and let the anger chemicals in his brain rebalance again. The TV seemed like an easy option. Jacob had mixed feelings about the news being on TV most of the day in the ward. It was good to feel connected to the world despite the three sets of thick doors and temperature checkpoint between him and the outside world. He did not like all the misery of the number of deaths seeping in and the remote was kept in the nursing station with nurses usually saying they were too busy to get it or just couldn't find it.

There was now news of the Black Lives Matter protests escalating in the US. Jacob wanted to be out there supporting the parallel movement of Blak Lives Matter by his mob. This Aboriginal movement focused on mistreatment and deaths in much worse facilities than the ward.

He asked Jessie for her stash of chalk and she helped him with a small and creative tribute to #BLM. They chalked 'George Floyd' and the number '432' representing the reported number of Aboriginal deaths in custody since a major 1991 inquiry.

Looking at the descending sequence of 4-3-2, he hoped it was like a countdown to the protests where there might be 1 more dramatic death that causes change to bring deaths to 0. It was more of a fleeting mathematical observation than a fully formed delusion but could have led to further seeking out of connections between themes in the world making associations about Black to Blak protests and the Black Death.

Before bed, Jacob heard chanting protestors like a dream, but they seemed to come from his sealed window. He looked out into the darkness and there was a lone man under a lamp post who appeared to mouth words that echoed into Jacob's mind: "you will come out of this, the bird spirits will rebalance". He reflected on how unlikely it was to hear anyone from this distance through thick safety glass but couldn't sleep as he internally debated whether he had special spiritual powers or was just crazy.

One of the therapists in a group session said you shouldn't stay in bed if you have insomnia but instead go do something relaxing and then return ready to sleep. There was not much to do except a couple of laps of the ward where he saw 'the Cuckoo'. She was seen by some as the most crazy on the ward but no one could really know how each person was internally reacting to trauma or illness. The Cuckoo was scribbling in crayon under the dim night lights. Jacob asked to look at it and the Cuckoo gave a yes-sounding grunt. It was all about how a vaccine would be used to control the world because of a secret merger between two big pharma and big tech companies. Some kind of nanochips in each injection had tiny antennas communicating as a mesh network globally linked via new 5G towers.

Even in Jacob's much more suggestible state, he could see how crazy this was but it was scientifically interesting still. It was a combination of beliefs held by many people who were not locked up and were not considered clinically insane because such a large sub-culture agreed on similar conspiracies. Why was Jacob expected to fit one model of what wellness was meant to look like for 'normal' people? He didn't want to be normal and didn't want to go back to the mundane baseline of his old life. Two voices in his head debated over 5G but the foolishness of the conspiracy and seeing it expressed by the Cuckoo reassured Jacob that he could still hold onto reality using evidence and logic. He might need others who had been through similar things to remind him of what is real.

Jacob was told he was being 'intrusive' by asking questions of other patients but then tried keeping to himself and got the label of 'isolative' in his notes -he couldn't win. He didn't even know how you could win at this game or what the rules were for getting out of hospital.

He started asking questions that helped profile each patient using bird names to code notes he wrote about people in his leather-bound journal. In the back of the journal he drafted equations of what it took for each patient to get discharged based on a subjective rating of their symptoms and supports in their community like carers or support workers as well as gender, likely risk of hurting someone, number of admissions and estimated age. There were obvious gaps in what information Jacob could gather where patients were private and because he could not always overhear what was said to doctors or nurses. Still there was a huge degree of randomness and contradictions in whether patients could leave or not. It seemed like placing mathematical logic on top of an inconsistent pseudoscience wasn't going to help Jacob figure out the rules of the game he was forced to play.

The next day the staff member Jacob like most explained what his role was again. He wasn't a nurse or therapist, but a Peer Worker - someone who had experienced his own severe mental distress but learned to overcome or at least manage it. Though many people have experience in the mental health system or as carers, Peer Workers learn how to use that experience in a supportive way and the better ones also bring out new stories and realisations from patients.

Jacob was also visited by a female Aboriginal Health team member but men's business, especially health was meant to come from another man. This would have happened if there were enough Aboriginal men working in mental health to cover the worker who moved into the 'Protect Your Mob' team to prevent the virus spreading to vulnerable indigenous communities.

Despite the lack of indigenous-specific support that was gender-appropriate, the Peer Worker named Mark help reorient Jacob away the goal of being cured and discharged to the goal of living well back home even if his symptoms continued.

Jessie didn't hear voices but was a good example of someone who kept fighting and progressing along a quest to learn and help others. Jessie's goals had seemed to flow out unpredictably, but this was usually because she sensed the course ahead was dangerous for her or those she was trying to help.

~ 10 ~

TEN

On what must have been about her hundredth phone call to the HomeLink homelessness service and without a clear reason was told she would now be taken on by Specialist Homelessness Services. It was a mystery why Jessie hadn't been referred to this service already as they have part of their focus on people with 'mental health issues'. Three free nights in a dumpy motel nearby would be given with the vain hope that it would be enough to find something more permanent.

The hospital had made basic but constant efforts to try get Jessie out in order to free up a bed. After a quick doctor's review, she laid out her few belongings along her bed and swept them up into a duffle bag like a pelican gathering fish into her bill. She hugged Jacob while reminding him his next review tribunal was only a few weeks away and he would be out soon. Jessie looked around at the ward that had become her home and the diversely scattered flock of other patients. The nurses had treated the ward like their territory, but they just came and went to their workplace. For Jessie and the others, it was a temporary but un-wanted home with not even any element of the natural world experienced across the last five months during the cancellation of all leave.

The motel was disgusting. There were many others on their three-night credit and vultures lurked nearby hoping to deal drugs to the vulnerable. Jessie was so glad to be out of hospital finally that she didn't want to do anything to jeopardise her recovery but was still deeply tempted to fill the craving for a high that remained at the back of her mind even though the chemical addiction was forced to disappear due to difficulties smuggling drugs into the ward. Ice was smoked on the ward by a few patients who would get the meth in foil from a visitor, light the foil with a lighter also smuggled in and suck in the smoke through a pen emptied of its cap and stick of ink. The effort of having to do all this was enough of a barrier to stop Jessie from using in the ward and now she was just strong enough to say no to a dealer who propositioned her on her way to a convenience store nearby.

If her day had been a little more difficult or even if she felt more in a celebratory mood for getting out of hospital, she would have taken whatever she could afford from the dealer. She now had more cash after a Welfare Officer helped her go from the standard unemployment benefit to a disability pension and saved a few extra supplement payments due to the virus. With no reason to spend money in hospital really except a loan repayment to her brother, Jessie realised she might blow her money away. Many other patients were forced to have a friend, relative or government agency manage their money but when they tried that on Jessie. A tribunal didn't have enough evidence to prove overspending as she tended to use cash more than transactions tracked in bank statements.

Jessie had $4,114, no fixed ties anywhere, and the strong belief that there must be some other place in the world who could help her fix her trauma so she could start to achieve some audacious goals. Melbourne seemed to have a much better mental health system with its inclusion of patients in more decision-making, but the city was deep into lockdown still.

She had heard that Finland in the 1980s had made huge advances with mental health and she pictured a village of snow-covered wooden cottages with smoke from their chimneys burning away all their problems. She drew it in her mind then made crude depictions with a stick in the dirt near the shops. Visualising this utopia, she drew Billy and Jacob there as her own goal involved helping others achieve theirs.

In her utopian vision in the dirt she drew a circle around the houses and people. There were mountains surrounding the houses, but they could be flown over. Then Jessie noticed that she almost involuntarily drew a circle around the whole drawing. Must have been some idea of a thought bubble or sense of one holistic vision for the future. Then she also randomly drew crown-like extensions out of the circle. It was the coronavirus shape -the toxicity had polluted her vision by clipping the wings of all flights in.

Melbourne and Finland were the only plans for next steps that day -clearly not a very helpful set of options to come out of one-third of the allowed motel time where she would have a definite roof over her head. She had used up all her favours for couches or mattresses in garages around Sydney and even with her savings and time in hospital for her social credits to reset, she decided to see a friend in Canberra. The nation's capital is infamously boring but maybe that's what she needed right now to regroup. She also heard that Canberra was a student town so looked at study options on her cracked screen.

Not realising that the two bus routes down to Canberra were inexpensive, Jessie booked a pensioner train ticket to get there instead. Her frugal habits would not disappear despite her current savings. Still, her generosity meant she gave away much more than her discounts to the many homeless people in the park near the station. Belmore Park had its many basic and small tents cleared out with major efforts in 2015 and 2017 with numbers going down again this year due to programs to prevent Covid among the homeless. Still, Jessie saw some familiar faces and her smile and empathetic conversation was worth more than the fivers she gave before anyone even asked for them.

Her homeless home girls thought she must still be crazy for wanting to go to cold and dull Canberra. "Can't go to Vic, can't go to Canberra but the border is still open to the 'Berra so I have no choice" remarked Jessie to the two ladies who seemed to have aged twice as fast as her.

Canberra was a city only built as a compromise between Melbourne and Sydney competing to have the capital there. They put the capital roughly in the middle of the two largest Australian cities -also the middle of nowhere. Canberra is land-locked and had only a small river that was dammed to become a lake in order to give the artificial impression of a harbour. In the local words of the Ngunnawal people, Canberra meant meeting place -perhaps a good omen for Jessie to meet important new people.

Jessie met her old friend Sal at the main Canberra station, and they caught up over lunch at a cafe along a fairly new precinct nearby called Kingston Foreshore. Sal knew Jessie used recreational drugs and they dropped a few pills together before, but this was the first she was hearing about all the hospitals and homelessness. Sal become worried about whether her friend might flip out and freak out the other two housemates in their four bedder in a suburb called Deakin. Sensing a change in body language, Jessie made genuine reassurances she would take her meds, not use drugs and not overstay her welcome.

Accustomed to going to bed at 9 as was routine for most on the ward, Jessie also woke up at dawn. She went to explore the neighbourhood and counted over 50 associations or non-profits just in one suburb. She didn't want to work for the rigid, slow and micropolitical public sector and not for corporates but running events for associations might be a good way to have a base in Canberra but still travel around when the borders reopened. She had ideas for more engaging large online events but local watch parties of those events to be a safer and cheaper way to get the benefits of face-to-face connection and more networks would be localised.

Instead of going for jobs, she drew out plans for the local/online hybrid model on a whiteboard in a library filming herself and sending it to associations she liked. Desperate for income, even in Canberra which was sheltered from most of the economic carnage experienced in places like Melbourne, two events managers invited Jessie in for an interview and she took the one with less pay but a better team. The Association for Australian Academics (AAA) was a pretentious sounding but had noble underpinning values. They were struggling to support university academics who mostly needed to reskill to teach more students online or suffer from the many cutbacks from lost revenue of international students.

Not having been to uni at all but aware of most universities' dependency on international students for over a third of income, Jessie could see how her work could help academics to better respond to the new normals of the video conferenced classroom and need to collaborate and disseminate research without travelling. Picturing this visually, she saw a global map with thicker borders than usual including some internal like the state of Victoria. Rather than fly out to partner with unis abroad or fly international students into Australia so much, she saw the web linking everything, but much denser local clusters linked to each other like hubs and spokes. Students could study at a local uni but get lessons from a more world leading research via video link and have their work marked locally but checked for quality some with strict accreditation. Though not a novel idea, she could see simpler ways to achieve this vision because she didn't carry the baggage of an indoctrinated bureaucracy limiting thinking.

As she started to fall asleep that night, the image in her mind of all the real-world local clusters and virtual links morphed. Her utopia of mental health services drawn in the dirt was like a real-world cluster of experts in research and treatment collaborating across many mental health disciplines. You would fly into this village virtually with people who support you also joining from wherever they were in the world. Treatment would be in short but frequent bursts and you would still have your local cluster of services, but they would be shared across government, private and charity sectors with less blocked up public psych ward beds. The hubs were there across the world, it was just about getting a coordinating HQ or clever system of collaboration to redirect flows of people, treatment options and data to flag illness before it becomes crisis.

As she laid her head for bed, she imagined a convergence of three rivers around a mountain to a utopia where birds nest among trees around houses of healthy people. She pictured this village with imagery from a travel show about a tourist trap in Lapland where kids could meet someone dressed as Santa Claus and feed some reindeer. The promise of better health in Lapland seemed as mythical as Santa who was said to live there when not at the North Pole. Still, Santa was a magical idea that brought meaning to believers and fond memories to many most who once believed.

The next day, Jessie caught a bus to the Parliamentary Triangle -always fairly devoid of people but now a few were emerging from lockdown and from a quasi-hibernation Canberrans go through in winter. Near the Triangle is the National Library where Jessie entered after a tea at the café.

She looked for various things hoping random search terms would spark ideas for work and for her own wellness journey. She came across a play called *The Eradication of Schizophrenia in Western Lapland* which sounded intriguing.

The play contrasted common treatment approaches for psychosis with a community-focused approach has evidence of positive outcomes in Western Lapland. Though 'eradication' was an overstatement, the play showed authentic concurrent narratives of the old way versus the innovative Finnish treatments. In Jessie's highly visual mindset the play came to life exactly as it read in a theatre critic's review:

> "The audience of *The Eradication of Schizophrenia in Western Lapland* enters one of two rooms with two sections of the play running concurrently on either side of a wall. The two rooms were connected by windows only covered with thin curtains so you could still faintly hear acting on the other side which blurred the two storylines together. In the second act, each half of the total audience switches sides and the full story is revealed including stark juxtaposition of treatment approaches. This innovative staging gives audiences a deep insight into what it is like to be psychotic."

Jessie was pissed off at this last bit as no one knew what it was like to be psychotic unless you experienced it firsthand. "Maybe we should give all the tickets to the show to doctors and put LSD in their pre-show champagne so they really know what it's like" joked Jessie to herself even though she would never do something so unethical or dangerous.

The community-focus of the Open Dialogue approach depicted in the play didn't seem to fit Jessie's lack of strong or fixed connections to a community. For Billy and Jacob though, it made a lot more cultural sense to engage extended family and broader cultural groups. The problem was that work first need to happen to destigmatise mental distress from these communities.

The term stigma was said to come from Ancient Greek meaning a marking or branding like one used on slaves or army deserters. As well as his truth tattoo, Jacob now had schizophrenia painfully and permanently inked into him every time he disclosed his illness to someone new. He also saw this ugly branding as if it were scarred into his right bicep because it resembles the opposite of truth: false delusions and an inability to fully trust his senses like when hearing voices that weren't real.

Jessie didn't feel the stigma of appearing as being from a minority race like Billy who now had the added stigma of the Wuhan-effect. Jacob passed as white but still carried the stigma of his indigeneity to white people who knew about it and occasionally stigma of a fairer complexion to his Koori mob.

Jessie did have the triple stigma of being a female, having a mental illness and being poor. Socioeconomic status could be masked somewhat with careful elocution and an expensive wardrobe. Mental illness was also a masked stigma like Jacob's bicep tattoo, but it is revealed like a raised sleeve when you look in the mirror as self-stigma and after a mandatory disclosure from certain employers.

Fortunately, the onboarding forms at AAA just asked, 'do you have any illness that might affect your performance at the Association?' Jessie didn't anticipate getting unwell again so could tick 'No' with a somewhat good conscience.

~ 11 ~

ELEVEN

Jacob's six-month Involuntary Patient Order had finally ended. Leading up to the Tribunal to decide whether he could be let out, Jacob used the ward tablet to research good things to say. He rehearsed what to say but as a set of clear and repeated themes rather than a script that would sound less authentic. He was not going to rely on a Legal Aid lawyer to advocate for him -it would be a different one this time than the one who helped Billy leave but failed Jacob. It was also a different junior doctor in the hearing as they rotate around.

Dr Stone instructed his junior to go for another six-month order which would mean Christmas in hospital and missing the first term of a new school year. He didn't focus on missing life outside in his arguments to the three tribunal members but made assurances of his safety and total compliance. Cherry assisted with more research on the elements of the Act related to her role as a carer.

"I acknowledge that I have schizophrenia but have recovered enough in hospital to manage my symptoms with medication and treatment. I feel like I am on the right medication now and will not take on too many stressful things so I can stay well. I will not make any major decisions without input from my wife and my mum" Jacob said in a careful and believable tone. "And I will check he takes the pills and go for walks each night to ask about how he feels" said Cherry sounding a bit more rehearsed than Jacob because she had planned out the statement to sound like formal English befitting a court appearance.

In the pre-Covid ward, patients were often given overnight leave in the lead up to a planned discharge to try out how things go at home without the supervision and structures of a ward. With the hospital still on the middle risk category of an Amber infection alert, very few patients got permission to leave and return to the ward due to the infection they might bring back that could quickly spread among people with issues that are comorbid with mental illness like obesity and diabetes. Without the trial run, Jacob was at risk of the shock of the transition leading to stress, relapse of acute psychosis and readmission back to this hospital or the ward close to his home.

Tribunal considered these matters as they adjourned briefly. On return from the deliberations, they agreed to a discharge but asked for a case manager from Jacob's local hospital to be arranged to see him regularly and highly recommended he not teach again until next year and then only then, as casual relief work. Though he felt this lawyer, psychiatrist and social worker in the tribunal had overstepped by trying to dictate a career plan, he hugged Cherry with glee. Voices in his head were only faintly there but sounded like they were having a party and the mean voice was left in the corner of the room mumbling about Jacob needing to stay in hospital.

On the top floor of their Liverpool apartment block out on his balcony overlooking the shopping centre, everything seemed just the way it was before. Everything except for how him now out of the fire but unsure if he was burnt all over or still had beautifully pure parts of his old self. It wasn't black and white: like the baby magpie whose grey turns either black or white, there was hope but still an ongoing transformation.

With the thoughts of birds, he daydreamed himself perching on the outdoor lounge then hopping up to the balcony railing and gliding down to eight-stories to sudden death below. He had no real intent to commit suicide but certain voices in his head became more persuasive, so he started to try to make deals with the angriest two voices.

"I can't talk to you right now so please don't bother me" he said aloud to the most evil-sounding voice. Another voice congratulated him for standing up to the bullying voice. The voice got angry so Jacob made a deal "I will talk to you at 7-8am and 7-8pm

laughing to himself at the apparent ridiculousness that an attempt to rationalise with an auditory hallucination might actually work. It didn't work this time but with repetition and support from therapists, this method of making verbal contracts with voices had strong evidence to work to dampen the persecutory voices for the majority of people who hear them.

Jacob then picked up his phone and dialled a six-digit number. "Life Callback Australia, how can we help?" a lady answered after seven long minutes on hold. "I'm on my balcony and I am not going to jump but just looking for some other way to stop the voices" reported Jacob. The Life Callback volunteer counsellor assessed this as higher level risk and was careful to first encourage him away from the balcony and then both identify and reorient Jacob's perceptions that he was a burden to Cherry and his mum and then started to shift his misconception didn't belong in the world any more.

The unnamed Life Callback counsellor said Jacob must go to Emergency if the feelings came back but, in this case, Jacob had probably stepped back from the edge of suicide safely. The suggestion to see a GP occurred straight away. The local Aboriginal Land Council ran the clinic where Jacob's Vietnamese Australian doctor practiced. They had returned to face-to-face consultations finally, were only a few blocks away and Dr Phan was prepared to see Jacob just after the clinic was due to close because he knew about the overlapping risks of suicide that were much higher for males, Aboriginal patients and those recently discharged from a psychiatric ward. It was a triple threat to Jacob's life but less concerning because Jacob had taken the important first step of seeking professional help.

On his way to the Aboriginal-owned clinic, Jacob recognised three people in the park opposite the clinic. They were injecting something in daylight hours with children around. Jacob was embarrassed that he knew these people and tried to avoid making eye contact.

"Jake you fucking dog, come over here and hang with your own mob for once instead of that little Thailand girl" said one Aboriginal woman smoking a cigarette. Jacob kept walking and added the names of those three to his Target List.

Jacob was a big fan of Dr Phan and knew he was in the lucky minority of Australians who got to see an empathetic and competent doctor quickly and nearby. With all the new telehealth options and GP search engine and booking apps, Jacob imagined some kind of technical integration to form the help-seeking branches of Billy's tree branching app that Jacob's mate Aroha and said was gaining real momentum and potential.

Dr Phan gave Jacob some of his own non-prescription Melatonin to help him rest and a prescription for eight strong benzos to curb the current intensity of the voices. With only eight pills, it would help avoid potential addiction but more importantly encourage Jacob to use some of the sensory self-soothing strategies like counting all green things he could see rather than take pills as the first line of defence to distress.

In what was either a weird coincidence or the universe re-acting to Jacob's thoughts, Billy phoned as Jacob left the GP clinic. "I've missed you mate" they said simultaneously and then laughed simultaneously. Their bromance was more intense than most because they had lived together in the close quarters of the ward and shared so many weird similarities and apparent epiphanies. Ignoring advice from the doctor about not staying close, the boys caught up on family, meds and what they had heard about Jessie. Then the topic of the tree app came up.

Was it shelved temporarily while Billy had work or cancelled completely? With the intellectual property clauses that some companies use to claim ownership of employee ideas, even those outside of hours, Billy was unsure. Jacob explained the possible link to the GP locator and booking systems which was well received and made Billy consider the possible application programming interface (API) to bring together his system with best in breed existing apps rather than reinvent every wheel of his new wellness vehicle. Getting men to realise the need to see their GP or other sources of help would be much more complex than the code linking each system.

Billy explained about his private psychiatrist and the slimy insurance-focused psychiatrist who pushed him to go back to work. It was clearly too soon for Jacob to be in front of 28 teenagers each class, but he needed something to do.

"Why don't we do this Tree app as a partnership? You can start as sole-trader and company founder then we restructure into a non-profit and I code a brand-new app from scratch after I quit so no one else owns the code" planned Billy to Jacob who was already feeling overwhelmed but excited by the possibility.

Billy was unaware that Cherry's paralegal work was actually in commercial law.

Cherry hesitated at dinner when asked whether she could help form the new company structure. She could easily structure the company as a charity, but Directors had a lot of legal responsibilities including potential criminal prosecution. Going broke was also more likely in the difficult economic situation created by the virus. She could see that old spark in Jacob though and knew he would probably just register the venture himself which might risk their personal finances if it was poorly structured.

After just a month the venture renamed to Well Tree was a registered corporation, with official charity status from the government and with Cherry, Jacob and Billy serving happily and legally as Directors. Cherry identified some grants for the pair to work on and kept meticulous financial records along with controls to stop bad purchases.

When he received the certificate of incorporation and again when he got Well Tree's charity registration certificate, he had a celebratory cigarette and bottle of decent McLaren Vale Shiraz. He knew that smoking made his anti-psychotic medication less effective so had cut down but still smoked as a special treat with alcohol which he also had less often than before his dramatic recent 'episode'.

He texted to share the news with pride to his dear mate Aroha. Billy and Aroha were still meeting up for contemplative walks with many concluding with a debrief at Jacob's house. On the balcony the three guys would share some of what they learned from deeply listening to each other and the thoughts nurtured by the natural serenity of Sydney's many walking paths. After the sixth balcony beer each, the three decided to track down Jessie and managed to find her under a pseudonym on Facebook so added her and called on Messenger.

"Here's trouble -three crazies drunk on a balcony. Sounds like the start of a bad joke" said Jessie from Canberra on video call. They positioned the phone on the outdoor table as if she was sitting with the other three. They all talked for hours with insights from Jessie's research on Finland's approaches to treatment peppered in to updates on Well Tree and sharing of the new digital representation of Jessie's original tree drawing.

With some of the state borders starting to re-open, Jessie told the guys that she was working hard on plans for an academic conference in Adelaide on online learning. Jessie noted Aroha's Kiwi heritage and explained that New Zealanders were allowed to fly in without quarantining. It was like Australia had acquired a long-lost state of New Zealand but lost the still isolative and even more insular Western Australia as a state where the conference was originally planned for.

One controversial academic from New Zealand was scheduled to speak on the impact of the virus on international student welfare. Billy then saw younger people like him as the logical pilot group for the app given universities could roll it out pretty quickly and adoption of new apps was often fast among uni students. Billy asked Jessie if he could have the couch of her hotel room in Adelaide and sneak into the conference just for this one plenary which she happily obliged.

Jacob could see the impact of the virus on his own students back in March. Although he couldn't see how Billy made the connection between Jessie's work and the planned app, he trusted that something positive for Well Tree's future users would come out of Adelaide. Prior to 2020, Jacob had always tried to set goals followed the SMART mnemonic of Specific, Measurable, Achievable, Relevant, and Time-bound. He particularly like the idea of measurable as was befitting a maths teacher and he would continue to follow in his management of the new venture.

Thinking about the current mess of the United States election, Jacob wondered how someone who so many Americans thought was dumb would become Leader of the Free World. If he was the exemplar of 'stable' and 'smart', there was hope for Jacob to reach the heights of leadership in any field.

After sobering up from the beers, he got out his small whiteboard and drafted a new idea of UNSMART goals. His new year resolutions for 2021 would be set according to a countercultural new approach he proposed as a guiding document for all future Well Tree employees. All goals were to be UNSMART in terms of being:

Unspecific: a clear overall vision but flexibility to pivot when new approaches are learned and unpredictable things like a new cluster or vaccination emerged.

Novel: an emphasis on new ways of doing things with unexpected outcomes so that goals must be updated when new approaches failed or yielded unexpected success.

Socially minded: with a move away from individual goals to goals that served Jacob, his community and the greater good.

Measurable: with simple metrics that directly relate to the clear overall vision or sub-goals that logically cascade out of the vision.

Audacious: each goal did not have to be realistically achievable as a harder goal would get better results and he would forgive himself if he fell short.

Relationship-based: planning for the fact that achieving goals is dependent on relationships which support those goals given that the 'lone entrepreneur' is a myth.

Tenacious: holding strong on the clear overall vision even with the arrival of novel approaches, input from relationships and pivots to a changing environment.

To check these ideas were logical, he thought he would teach them to Cherry. Preparing to teach a topic and then teach it are rumoured to be the best ways to remember and understand complex principles. Cherry loved the idea and thought it was quite marketable like an 'Unconvention' she had attended that sparked a lot of interest among her colleagues who respected the need for new ways of working.

Jacob's first UNSMART goal was not to launch an app but to create a resource that helps improve mental health in Australia. If they pivoted away from apps or even from any form of digital resource, the unspecific overall vision could still be pursued.

While planning for the future, Jacob also made a brief visit to his lawyer to prepare his last will and testament. He wasn't yet sure when his family might need this but imagined his body being painted with traditional white body point and then his burial on some inevitably rainy day.

~ 12 ~

TWELVE

Adelaide didn't have as bad a rep as Canberra for being boring but on both Billy's Sydney to Adelaide flight and Jessie's Canberra to Adelaide flight, they overheard someone saying it was
a long descent because Adelaide was such a hole. That month
though, a major survey had just found Adelaide to be the most
liveable metro areas in Australia. Melbourne was usually seen
as the most liveable city but that seemed ridiculous to survey
respondents while Melbourne had so many infections and was
trapped inside one of the world's most strict lockdowns.

Billy met Jessie at the lobby of a hotel near the *Karrawirra
Parri* / Torrens River. The familiar hug and quick return to the
warmth of such a close friendship led the two down *Karrawirra
Parri* past the conference venue and to a restaurant where they
had a few too many Proseccos. They decided to go to the local
gay bar after as they had a night of drag show tributes. The two-
story club was in a back-alley heritage building and the crowd
were unfriendly but not as bad as most other venues in what was
also the meth capital of Australia.

It was just vodka and energy drinks for the pair but there was
an aura of impending doom that Billy could sense but Jessie ig-

nored. Jessie was being creepy with gay guys with no intention of hooking up but just being close and cheeky like she was when her gay friends once gave her the derogatory label of 'fag hag'. The Adelaide scene seemed even more bitchy than those Sydney snobs and Billy had to intervene when the club closed at 3am and Jessie yelled at some skinny twink boy who minced around the club like he was the only queen there.

Some of the clubbers kicked on to one of the only places still open and serving alcohol -the casino. Billy cringed and saw the risks of being that drunk in a casino at this hour so handed Jessie over to one of the random's care as Billy took her hotel key and walked back for a short sleep.

On his way back through Rundle Mall, Billy was busting to pee and asked some police where he could find a toilet. "There's some disgusting ones on North Terrace near the uni but cleaner ones in the casino" said the constable who made Billy recall the terrible night where police cornered him in an alley similar to where he had just been. Opening his phone on the last bar of battery, Billy saw the casino and was fairly close but he then spewed up some the night's vodka in disgust that a cop could recommend he go to the casino at this time of night in such an obviously drunken state.

He eventually headed in the right direction of the hotel. On his way some old guy propositioned him. After claiming he was a millionaire for selling shares, the disgusting man grabbed Billy's arse but was quickly pushed away. The man laughed and said he something so vulgar that Billy wanted to find the police again.

Seeing this interaction from across the street, some local bogan called Billy a 'fucking poof' and threatened to kill him. It was not an idle threat. The man was luckily even more drunk than Billy and his 10-minute effort to chase Billy through streets he knew much better than the Sydney boy, led him to tire out and scream homophobic hate speech to no one in particular.

Worried about Jessie in her drunken, irritable and overly energetic state and in a city with douchebags like the homophobic bogan, he got out his phone to call her, but the battery had just gone dead.

The stress of organising the conference under more difficult global conditions than any event manager had ever seen combined with the lack of sleep was a recipe for disaster. Jessie should have gone back to the hotel at 3am when it closed, if not well before then.

The casino in the early hours of Saturday morning was full of people trying to get in the last few rounds of drinks and a big win before the casino closed at 6am. It would open again at 9am but the brief closing period meant people were in a bigger hurry to waste their money on the tables, pokies and more drinks.

The virus had only slightly lessened the crowds in the casino with token efforts to enforce 1.5m social distancing requirements. Out in the smoking area Jessie bought a pack to share with others as she knew that a shared cigarette was a great way to meet people and just one or two smokes given to others would cheer them up. As she wasn't a regular smoker, the few cigarettes and clouds of smoke in the area unventilated by the still winds of the morning made her cough and have a sore throat. She got greasy looks as she coughed by older Karens but the chilled-out smokers just suspected smokers' cough.

A tall man in the corner of the area was playing a rave track which Jessie recognised as a rave DJ -a favourite of hers when she was a teen. She was surprised that anyone still played his Hard Dance sets, let alone randoms in Adelaide well outside the DJ's hometown of Sydney. The tall guy shuffled like an emu clawing along sand with his head quickly vibing to the fast beat.

His flared pants were straight out of Jessie's memories of raver boys shuffling back and forth in random fields or warehouses.

Noticing Jessie's vibing was synchronised with his own, the emu approached and they both reminisced about the rave scene which was apparently still vibrant in Adelaide. Getting along ridiculously well, the two gathered even more strangers in an ad hoc dance floor that might have seen Jessie put away if anyone knew how manic all the excitement was making her.

As it was a small city and the casino had a few scumbags, it was not a huge coincidence that the man who had chased Billy that night showed up. This was despite his obvious inebriation that would have set a breathalyser to a point that would shock even avid fans of the TV show RBT. He ordered a rum and cola even though he was too drunk to be legally allowed to drink more or even be in a licensed venue.

From the other end of the bar to Jessie the drunk said "I love chubby girls" in a slurred squawk. Jessie piped up and called him a "fucking disgusting creep" which led the man to scream and approach her ready to push her fat arse to the ground. Security came quickly but the bartender blamed Jessie for the name-calling and she was dragged out of the casino with a ban from the venue for the typically low threshold of 24 hours.

The emu's friend from the smoking area saw it unfold and she offered to stab the drunk for Jessie. Jessie's quickly and politely declined. Jessie had never had someone over to stab a man for her, but it was a serious offer that she found very disturbing. Another passer-by overheard and claimed he was a lawyer who could help Jessie sue the casino for what had happened or at least advocate for more responsible service of alcohol and better safety for women.

Jessie loved the attention and wanted to talk to as many strangers as possible but she knew all this energy and activity was a big red flag. She may have already entered a manic phase of schizoaffective disorder or bipolar I -still unsure of which diagnosis made the most sense, if any.

Rather than call an ambulance given that South Australia might have similar laws as her home state in regard to ambulance arrivals leading to involuntary treatment, Jessie asked where the closest public hospital was. She intended to ride share there. The major hospital turned out to be just over a kilometre away and on the same street as the casino so she walked. The largest public hospital in the state was an imposing 800 bed budget overrun constructed just three years prior to Jessie's clumsy efforts to find the ED.

Despite being the 26th most expensive building in the world in nominal terms or 2nd most expensive building in the whole country in inflation-adjusted terms, the hospital completely failed to offer any form of care to Jessie. At this stage, Jessie was actually at a hypomanic state which might not have got more serious and turned into mania or full-blown psychosis. If the right PRN was given and she got a lift back to the hotel, she could potentially avert a crisis. Instead, Jessie followed the most tragically laughable sequence of events that perhaps anyone will ever have in a building worth over $2 billion:

1. Arrive at the 'Eastern entrance' which is closest to the city, but doors are locked, and no one was around
2. Use the intercom answered by security who give an overly vague explanation of how to get to the ED as 'to the West and down the road'
3. Use Maps to see which way west actually was but still get confused

4. Call the ED who got frustrated with Jessie as she walked the wrong way
5. Follow one of the very few signs to finally reach the ED
6. Get screened for temperature but the reading was so low she would have been clinically dead
7. Ask the Triage Nurse for a PRN to help with sleep because she had missed her regular medication
8. Get asked by the triage nurse "what is a PRN?"
9. Be turned away from ED totally and taken to a security guard who showed an interactive map of the vast hospital campus
10. Be recommended to go to a help desk back near the entrance as the map kiosk printed a little map with directions
11. Follow those directions up a lift, through a carpark, past a magpie mural, through a palatial food area and lobby and to the desk marked on the map
12. Find out that the help desk is staffed by volunteers who don't work on weekends and wouldn't be there if it were this early on a weekday either
13. Call Billy and Life Callback with the hope that a carer and a charity could provide better support while Jessie sat in an expensive and seemingly useless public facility

Even pre-Covid, it had turned out that the whole hospital had failed to handle some teething issues, but this was failure that even a pandemic would not excuse. Jessie thought of the cough-shaming Karens as she coughed from the night of too much smoke inhalation for someone not used to it anymore. A Junior Doctor clocking on to her morning shift overheard the cough and demanded that Jessie go to the flu clinic so she waited another three hours in a hospital that she thought could have spent a billion less on fancy construction to actually fund more competent and empathetic staff. Better staff would probably end up saving money by acting before a health concern became a health crisis.

Jessie asked one of the nicer clinic nurses to get her hotel to page Billy who arrived soon after in a black face mask just-in-case. No one in the clinic recognised the clear signs of mental distress. As the two wandered back from the hospital to the hotel, their facial masks strained their breathing. This reminded Billy of the breathing techniques of long in-breaths but even longer out-breaths. It was easy for Billy to check Jessie was doing it right as her blue mask deflated and inflated slightly. It took many tries to slow her breathing down but Billy mimicked the careful and patient efforts of Aroha listening and watching for tiny changes to his friend's breathing patterns and then gently correcting them.

Perhaps this could be a simple feature of the Well Tree app -just a breath counter. It was in some of the mindfulness apps, but they were starting to become less trendy except with the loyal fringe who originally embraced the bastardised forms of Chinese meditation. The counter could be a bit more advanced than an expanded and contractor circle he saw on one app and instead reward the user with points or badges.

It was no time to be pondering the app, but Billy knew that those responding to an emerging crisis like this also need to work on self-care. The distraction of the app and calming thoughts about how many people the Well Tree charity could benefit helped Billy to then re-focus completely on planning Jessie's pathway away from the edge of madness. Was she already past the threshold of needing professional support or could he bring her back?

Billy encouraged, then persuaded Jessie to book a phone consult with her GP in Canberra. She was worried the doctor might call an ambulance in Adelaide somehow. The GP instead keen for a quick fix in the form of a PRN prescription faxed straight to a chemist a block away from the pair. They filled the script right away, Jessie took the maximum dose and by the time they were back in the hotel room, all felt well again.

The mania was still there, and psychosis was now setting in. These symptoms were concerning but did not present an immediate danger. Jessie didn't hear voices and the pills had meant she was less likely to take risks because she did not have the same manic energy as before. The two lay on the king size bed next to each other and Jessie was thankful to have Billy guide her along the path from madness back to wellness.

Billy hooked up a small device to a port of the TV and started to play Ellen -a secret shame of the pair despite evidence of a toxic work culture at the show. Billy was getting the videos from the web and casting them to the TV which wasn't new to Jessie but seemed like he had hacked the hotel entertainment system or something. As Billy went to the bathroom his friend was now acting like she was in a dream. Jessie started to hear Ellen say 'Jessie, look at the camera in Billy's phone, we are taping auditions for the next appearance on the show using a new feature of the app.' Jessie was wide awake and really thought she heard these words but Billy couldn't hear the TV while the sink ran.

In the marble bathroom Billy was holding his breath briefly while splashing his face with cold water to trigger the 'dive response'. This simple method worked to refresh and relax people and animals by reducing heart rate and moderating blood circulation (through peripheral vascular resistance) to move blood flow more into the brain and heart instead of muscles not needing the blood as much. Through hacking the conditions of his body's internal environment (homeostatic control), Billy also re-balanced his mind to be ready to help Jessie for just long enough to help her divert away from another hospital stay.

When finding Jessie was trying to talk to Ellen from bed, he knew the room needed to be a low stimuli environment like hospital but with efforts to introduce sensory stimuli to distract then soothe. He started to cast some videos from a search of transcendental meditation not knowing that sometimes meditation and mindfulness can make delusions and paranoia worse because thoughts are left to intensify in quiet contemplation. Still, it was better than hospital where having random shows played and nurses rarely gave you the remote even if violent news or movies came on that would clearly trigger some unwell patients while also being bad energy for the ward overall.

The image of a blue background and red brain radiating energy had a sense of three-dimensional depth for Jessie. To her, the colours looked like new shades of blue and red that no one had ever seen before. The colours seemed to leap out of the screen toward her like 3D fractals synchronised with each beat of the soft music. The vibrations of the music felt like tingles on the fine hairs of her arms -like a tactile hallucination. Then she could smell something awful like Billy had done some dirty business in the bathroom. This was phantosmia – an olfactory hallucination of a phantom smell which of the rare people who experience it, the smells are usually disgusting and hard to identify if in an already smelly hospital.

The overlapping and false sensory experiences were still there while Billy rummaged through the mini bar to find things Jessie could use for sensory self-soothing. "Take this small bottle of orange and mango juice Jessie" he said in a way that intrigued her. "Notice the label, where it was made, the colours on it, what materials are used in the bottle, lid and label" he said as Jessie realised he was trying to guide mindful observation in such a se-rious way that it actually made her chuckle. "Now before you open the metal lid, feel the dimple in the lid, the texture of the glass and as you open the lid, listen to it pop and feel the dim-ple now in its different shape" guided Billy. Seeing that the med-itation video was distracting, Billy stop the cast and continued by saying: "smell the juice, what fruit is there and can you smell how sweet it is?" and Jessie nodded twice. "Now taste a small sip, what temperature is it, what is the likely ratio of orange to mango?" he continued. The two let out an audible sigh together which expelled just enough stress for them to help them start to decide what to do next.

Billy had been looking at loft apartments in the inner city back in Sydney as it was now time to move out of his parents' house even though they were useful for watching for signs of potential relapse. He asked Jessie if she would ditch the confer-ence and fly to Sydney to stay in either of the two lofts Billy had applications in for. Luckily, the swab result came back within eight hours because pathology had few tests to process that day. The pair risked a potential mental health crisis 35,000 feet in the air -luckily the flight was under two hours.

In the line boarding the plane, the two nearly got stopped by the federal police at the gate when Jessie made a loud comment about hoping she didn't have a total mental breakdown mid-flight. The two laughed it off like it was a euphuism and Jessie looked directly into the eyes of the police officer and mouthed "my time of the month sorry". As a second white lie soon after, Jessie texted her boss and said she was quarantining in the hotel waiting for a swab result -an easy lie many workers had used that year and she had the clinic attendance certificate in any case.

The flight was manageable with the pair taking a quick nap. Jessie was noticeably still unwell because she talked more than usual to those sitting nearby and spoke about deep topics uncommon to discuss with strangers.

Billy treated Jessie to a five star near a hospital that Billy had heard was slightly better than the one they had been to together that year. They had escaped Adelaide and the incompetence of recent ED nurses meant Jessie was not scheduled for involuntary treatment interstate but might still need hospitalisation in Sydney. Billy was ready to make that call when needed.

~ 13 ~

THIRTEEN

As the two woke that rainy Sunday, the world had lost 1.3 million people to the virus. That was like the whole population of Adelaide being killed over a 12-month period. At the conclusion of the conference that Jessie missed, anyone who stayed for short holidays like weekend vineyard trips ended up being caught in Adelaide's biggest virus cluster. They had three consecutive months without any new cases, but toilet paper sales and other panics spiked quickly and without much warning.

Though the cluster was small by global standards, it alarmed the whole of Australia and crippled Adelaide with an even harsher lockdown than Melbourne's. Due to misinformation provided to a Contact Tracer, the Adelaide November 2020 cluster turned out not to be as bad as authorities initially thought. Still, it rippled through the Australian psyche to make people wonder when the next cluster and lockdown might bubble up from infection sources like quarantined travellers.

Jessie was honest to her boss about the negative result but said she was symptomatic so could not assist with the conference. Someone from the conference venue filled in and praised Jessie for her meticulous run sheet and many diagrams explaining how the conference was to run. She dodged a bullet and kept her job.

The next few days were a gradual transition from Billy's small room to his new loft apartment in Pyrmont near work. They decided together on a Zen Japanese style for the loft while Billy imagined bringing men, women or non-binary hook-ups home and not correcting them when they assumed, he was Japanese rather than Chinese. Billy bought a pansexual pride flag from an online store which was a tricolour of vertical stripes of pink, yellow and blue. It was the only real splash of colour in the loft except for the browns of all the timber furniture, green of two bonsai trees and the layers of colours in the abstract paintings on the walls.

"Does pansexual mean you are attracted to pans?" Jessie joked as she held up a frypan that they bought that day for a greasy fry up. "Pan is from Ancient Greek [πᾶν] meaning all, everything, or everyone" replied Billy totally unimpressed with Jessie's attempt at humour. Regaining a sense of humour is actually a good sign of becoming well again unless the jokes are unusual or laughing is unusually inappropriate. "So, you will hook-up with anyone?" which Billy laughed along at knowing that he had been a man-slut in the past but was still angry that Jessie didn't understand this important aspect of his identity. Pansexual for him meant he was attracted to certain people no matter what their gender identity or gender expression but was now highly selective on who he might date.

"Maybe I'm panpolar or transpolar -I experience all sorts of moods and emotions including multiple at one time sometimes like fluid or nonbinary gender" said Jessie with a renewed logic that others may have seen as out-of-character and a sign of being unwell. It was an even more fringe view than the idea that we need 64 distinct terms to adequately explain the plethora of diversity in contemporary understandings of gender identity and expression.

Perhaps the American (DSM) and WHO (ICD) revised diagnostic criteria for mental illness could become much more varied and inclusive of diverse experiences of mental distress and on-going illness. These manuals could allow for more overlapping diagnoses and less emotionally charged clinical labels.

Though the colours of the pansexual flag didn't seem to go together and certainly didn't match anything else in the apartment, Billy found a large wooden frame as a border for it to mount it on the exposed brick walls. It was like roping off his diversity in a way that his sexuality did not totally define his identity.

Billy always wanted a cat so the two went to an animal shelter to rescue one. They chose a two-year-old cat who had just birthed kittens. They renamed the cat from Mumma to Y for Yin and Yang like her black and white fur. They made dad jokes directed at the cat the whole way home like 'Y, are you so cute?' and many starting with 'Y did the cat cross the road?'

'Y *didn't* the cat cross the road Billy?' asked Jessie who was still not tired of lame jokes. 'Because he was pussy!' was the cringe-worthy punchline.

Moving into and furnishing a new apartment was always going to be stressful. Jessie was still thinking and saying weird things but reporting to her GP every few days and giving Billy permission to call the mental health crisis team if he felt overwhelmed with worry for her.

Y was a perfect companion for Billy and kept Jessie. The cat helped them focus on a daily routine caring for her and helping the new fur baby to settle in. Y climbed the loft stairs and surveyed her new domain. The longhaired domestic's favourite spot was under the bed, but she had many other spots she liked.

She was a curious creature and quickly synchronised her own behaviours with the changing mood of both Jessie and Billy. If Jessie acted a bit hyperactive, Y would scurry around as if she were alerting her human aunty to a change in the overall energy in the house. If the cat's father Billy would come home stressed from work, she would sit on his lap and leave behind her black and white hairs on Billy's mostly black and white clothes as if he were to carry reminders of her wherever he went.

Billy further diverted Jessie's attention to a set of purposeful activities styling his place with no mucking around looking at different shops or comparing prices. They would buy most items from just one store – a Japanese minimalist store. Billy chose something Zen and relaxing for each of the senses with things like incense sticks for smell and intricate but minimal rugs and cushions with patterns to track along with your eyes. He also bought a bead sofa that was like a fancy bean bag with a tan denim texture on the outside, gentle massage as the beads move inside and auditory experience as the beads pressed together.

gokan

In the Japanese store, Jessie also bought copied pencils, triangular ballpoint pens of different colours and a range of stamps. She used these for visual journaling of daily changes in her mood and documenting what wellness strategies suited her. Apparently, shopping was also therapeutic when you removed the stress of shopping around and found stores that matched your style closely. She would pay attention to changes in mood with a stamp to represent each a mood on a scale of four: down, fine, great, and up. Other stamps also linked each journal entry with one or more emotions and as she reflected on past entries, she decided to repeat activities with the stamps she selected to represent emotions related to happiness or curiosity.

Jessie also started drafting mock complaint letters to people like the head of public hospitals in South Australia about her failed attempt to admit herself. If she sent them, she might be dismissed as a crazy Karen, but she imagined one day having the right connections and words to properly fix all the holes in the two states and one territory where she had lived.

After a week of rest, shopping and walks around Darling Harbour and Barangaroo Point while Billy was at work, Jessie felt well enough to send through some ideas to her manager for the Academic Forum coming up early in the new year. She suggested a sub-theme of the conference on mental health of faculty after the survey data on the student welfare plenary showed a growing interest in the mental health challenges of remote learning. Academics did not have the same financial challenges and lack of family supports faced by their international students but if they were more aware of their own wellness, they might also be role models for good stress-management techniques to students. The pressures to publish did not ease while academics had to move all content online and learn new ways of teaching and assessing remotely.

Jessie decided she was well enough to go back to work in Canberra and Billy reluctantly agreed. She booked a bus one-way for a Sunday afternoon and nearby the bus station was a men's mental health BBQ that Billy found on a group meeting website. The men and a few female friends or partners met at one of over thirty locations around the country with Billy choosing Surry

Hills because he knew a gay guy who went there. Billy needed a new tribe who could share their experiences of illness and wellness but weren't so unwell themselves that they were unable to help him back.

On the coach down Jessie looked for events and groups. She wanted to meet new people and get informal social support. Canberrans often lacked this support initially as the population was transitory and newcomers often formed friendship groups within their workplaces at government departments so topics like mental illness would be difficult to disclose to friends.

Always one for taking on too many new projects, Jessie planned to start her own women's wellness groups. Like the BBQ had kept the guys focused on social support rather than clinical support, she drew a scene of eight women on a Wellness Walk for Women (WWW) group idea in her Japanese-made sketchbook. She made herself a little thinner like a vision of how she might look after doing so much walking. Then, she planned out the promotion and scheduled locations of each walk in her 2021 diary with a focus on how each week might be themed around one of the five senses.

Women and men still have unique interests and approaches to getting help and talking about emotions. Jessie had noticed Billy had started to balance wellness approaches she perceived as feminine with masculine ones. His interior decorating was feminine as far as hobbies and professions are usually classed but he also still played video games like young men. The two are very different sensory experiences but while his urban sanctuary settled him down, his shooting games released aggression and connected him with online friends by audio. The two dancing games kept him fit with sweaty sessions as his cat matched the frenetic energy by running around the makeshift dance floor. Even how Billy interacted with that cat was a more feminine experience as he cared for her and stroked her like a good mother.

Jessie wanted to learn more about how all genders dealt with their problems so looked for other activities on top of her WWW group. She found a mental health 'story slam' called *The Brave*. The event was like a poetry slam but with stories of wellbeing and illness. It was established in the US and hosted plays and storytelling nights across several US states. Canberra was the heart of the Australian branch and came onto Jessie's radar via a news article about clothes they had secured with a few partner organisations to help people with a mental illness struggling with finances.

Jessie loved when her passions interlinked, and *The Brave* was at the nexus of her love of running events, helping people on incomes, and alleviating mental distress. It was like the interlinked Venn circles of the car logo again. At an open mic event, Jessie found her brave spirit and shared what happened in Adelaide. An Academic who was a member of the AAA where she worked happened to be in the audience and disclosed the worst parts of that story to Jessie's boss out of apparent concern for the association rather than just malicious gossip.

Canberra was a small place and as Jessie tidied up her desk for failing to declare the illness and make false claims about her sick leave, others in the office speculated and the story spread across the town in ways that were mostly only half-true. Jessie felt relieved that she had been open about the story but was pissed that someone in the audience would snitch on her. She was also furious when Cherry explained that while she could still complain about Unfair Dismissal within 21 days of being terminated and also complain to the Human Rights Commission for disability discrimination, she was partly in the wrong for the false declarations and bending of the sick leave system. She could have got broadly-worded medical certificates at the time and not disclosed what her illness was.

Her friend Sal felt bad but asked Jessie to move out of the share house unless she could quickly find a job and undo some of the gossip damage done by her noble but stupid disclosure. The flipside of the gossip chain was that those with their own lived experience as mental health carers or consumers rallied around Jessie. *The Brave* CEO heard about what happened and linked Jessie in with his many contacts in the events management game. An older man from her story slam audience who was bereaved by the suicide of his wife offered his granny flat rent-free for two months.

The universe was watching out for Jessie but was conspiring against others in her life for no apparent reason. As a semi-conscious sixth sense, Jessie felt an ominous sense of impending doom. Later as she walked along Lake Burley Griffin near her new granny flat in Yarralumla, she saw the carcass of a mute swan on the banks with three black swans out in the water. They each faced their dead cousin like they were grieving its loss -a strange interpretation of what she could see that she knew not to be true. Still the thought was useful in helping her process this tragic scene.

$$\sim 14 \sim$$

FOURTEEN

Cherry was working from home so she could keep a close eye on Jacob's recovery and have walks along the river with him at lunchtime. The 1pm walks after a light lunch were a nice relief from all the bankruptcy cases emerging out of Covid economic carnage. Cherry was working 11 hours a day on average.

For Jacob, the river walk brought a feeling of embarrassment and uneasiness with the memory of his strangely gamified experience. He still had positive memories of previous walks and Cherry's continued optimistic pace. The mix of happy and sad memories of places was like the black Yin leaching into the white Yang to upset an equilibrium. Cherry walked alongside her husband not ever walking in his shoes and never knowing what hospital was really like. Still, she had experienced her own pain from Jacob's journey which she rarely spoke about because she knew it was much worse for him.

Cherry turned to Buddhist chanting, guided meditation podcasts and the occasional trip to a large temple in Wollongong -south of Sydney. The vegetarian meals there led her to stop eating meat even though she longed for pork initially. It was easier to avoid pork around their neighbourhood of Liverpool-Fairfield as many restaurants are halal -even some Thai and burger joints. She also joked that Jacob should stop eating chicken given his love of birds.

She rang the giant bell on a hill in the temple grounds one day after a tasty tofu meal. She glanced down at the pagoda and contemplated the possible death of Jacob, but the thought quickly faded when she saw the winding path downhill to the main temple. The smell of incense wafted toward her and felt like an antibacterial cleanse combined with memories of Cabrogal smoking ceremonies that acted as purification rituals.

On the way back from the river, children of many complexions were playing in a water park that they could enter freely after school in the increasingly warm Western Sydney weather. They both thought again about whether they would have children despite the small risk of hereditary psychosis. They strolled past Liverpool Hospital where Jacob might end up if he replaced but at least they could walk there together from home if warning signs were noticed before ambulance or police might be needed.

On the metal cladding of the hospital wall, Jacob noticed a liver bird on the top left of the coat of arms shield. It was a bit like the Liverpool FC liver bird logo. It was next to a version of a caduceus -the traditional symbol of Hermes and the medical profession involving snakes winding up what was usually a staff but seemed in this coat of arms like it wound up a figure of a caring person. The details in the symbols and meaning behind them would have ordinarily been missed but Jacob's unusual thoughts earlier that year had woken up to a creative and poetic mindful way of thinking but potentially also to a sequence of deep thinking that eventuated in another break from reality. Below the bird and caduceus was a Waratah which was another case of bad memories bleeding into good ones. Jacob had memories of native Waratahs in dense shrub with one particularly vivid memory of a red wattlebird on a red Waratah. That memory in nature was now polluted with awful memories of the state government logo scattered round the hospital and on official letters making awful diagnoses official or on the letterhead of bills for the hospital after the first three months free period.

Jacob decided to get private health insurance as they walked past the small private hospital with its own psych ward. Getting a bed fast enough to be helpful might be difficult in private so Liverpool ED was still part of his crisis management plan -hopefully with no Covid cases there if and when it would happen. Cherry would have visited more if Jacob had been a local hospital but that would have come with its own burden of the time commitment and contagion of misery from seeing Jacob at his worst and overhearing complaints of other patients.

Back in their apartment, piles of paperwork on Cherry's desk towered over her like the half-empty skyscrapers of the city. Most were debtor's petitions -the form used for voluntary declaration of your company's bankruptcy. Each one documented miserable bankruptcy of companies with jobs lost to an economy with only 1 job ad for every 13 people looking for a job. If she couldn't get through this stuff without letting it totally upset her, she might never become a fully qualified lawyer.

Cherry could see how many termination letters would soon come from liquidators. Sometimes debts reported were just a few thousand dollars for the smaller businesses but just couldn't be paid given that the temporary business closures led to immediate insolvency then bankruptcy. She suspected there was an even bigger wave of bankruptcies coming as the first wave. She saw attempts at tax breaks and payments to jobseekers and supplements to salaries so businesses kept staff as positive. These trickles of payments might not stop the upcoming waves of destruction from further unemployment causing less spending and defaulting on bills such as rent.

A childlike voice in Jacob's head whispered to him "how is that busy woman going to raise crazy children like me?". Jacob asked for an update on his wife's plans for children and whether they could just adopt as it was more socially responsible and less likely for anyone to blame his 'defective' genes if anything went wrong. "I want our own kids, let's have some genetic tests or something" said Cherry trying not to escalate the confrontation but still engage in assertive problem-solving.

There are currently no genetic tests to screen for risk of hereditary psychotic disorders. Given causes of first episode psychosis were a constellation of genes, drug-use, past trauma and other environmental factors, a test for probability of an unborn child developing a mental disorder might be a long way off.

Looking on one of his video streaming services for some sort of documentary on hereditary genes or mental illness in families, Jacob stumbled on a supernatural horror. *Hereditary* was a 2018 movie detailing how mental illness in a family led to many deaths. Decapitated bodies possessed by demons were not great themes for Jacob right now and he read that one of the actors from the film had ongoing trauma from the horror acting experience.

Pop culture portrayals of mental illness are still highly stigmatising and almost always inaccurate. The horror genre was particularly bad at misusing mental illness as a way to advance plots on homicide, suicide or both. Even news stories get things totally wrong while reporting in a way that can deeply scar stigma into those with symptoms. This prevents help-seeking and the depictions of asylums as even worse than they are, prevents many from calling police or ambulance when they are really needed.

Jacob started to believe a voice in his head calling him a murderous maniac. He pleaded with Cherry to let him go to the RSL Club for one beer and a slap on the pokies. It was totally uncharacteristic of him to want to gamble because he knew how bad the odds were and even the more skill-based games of poker didn't entertain him.

Cherry didn't try to control her husband. Still, she carefully explained why it wasn't a good idea to go out. She then left it there because she didn't want their arguing about children to re-escalate into a bigger theme of monopolising all their decisions such as stopping the small sums wasted on alcohol and a rather unlikely new gambling habit.

At 4.44am, Aroha and Billy got the same text:

> "Jacob never came home last nite We argued & he went to RSL. Police won't do anything yet, do u know where he is?"

Aroha arrived in Liverpool first and Billy was not much longer. They both hugged and reassured Cherry but knew that a man with schizophrenia wandering off while still recovering from a recent episode was risky.

Out on the balcony away from earshot of Cherry, Aroha guessed that he might have gone walkabout. Billy was glad a half-Aboriginal suggested this because it was in his mind but seemed culturally insensitive to suggest. During Jacob's only walkabout in his mid-teens, he had walked 1000 miles, survived on bush tucker and drunk straight from streams. The practice was uncommon now and the term walkabout was often used by white people in a negative way as if Aboriginal people were still nomadic and randomly disappeared all the time like they were unreliably flaky.

The closest thing Billy had come to a Walkabout was on pub crawls in London where he often visited crass Australian-themed pubs of the same name. Even the pub crawl seemed to have more structured predictability of duration and location than Billy's understanding of indigenous Walkabouts but he dare not echo this idea to Aroha.

"Could we track his credit card?" asked Billy to Cherry who had already looked at their joint account and saw $3,000 withdrawn at the RSL. She later called them when they reopened at 9.30am but they were not prepared to give out information about a member except to police.

Billy knew it was a bit unethical but asked to see Jacob's history in Chrome. Luckily, it was signed in across multiple accounts so Billy could see searches across the laptop there and his phone. A search had been made just under an hour ago for a bird sanctuary.

Looking for birds was a strange think to do in the early morning after a rough night but at least it didn't seem risky. The next entry was more concerning, 'how to make Leilira blades' was the search phrase referring to a traditional Aboriginal knife. Could he want to hurt himself, hurt others or hunt like a Walkabout with this symbolic knife?

Later that day, spent from the lack of sleep while worrying about her husband, Cherry noticed an app purchase for a platinum dating app subscription. She couldn't believe that Jacob would want to cheat on her, he just wasn't like that. Maybe the voices were taking over his mind with sexual thoughts.

The dating app used location as part of its matching algorithm so Billy wondered whether police could find him through that or the telco records of locations matched to data, SMS or phone calls. He messaged Jacob many times, as did Aroha and Cherry but it might look to Jacob like they were all taking Cherry's side.

After stressful hours catastrophising on where he might be and what his voices might order him to do to hurt himself or others, the three decided to split up and go out looking for him. They checked with Liverpool ED, Police, the usual parks, and the shopping centre -nothing.

Thinking about times when he lucked out on all the dating apps, Billy called the massage parlours to ask if they'd seen him. One said they didn't give out that information but he charmed three others who sounded like they had seen someone similar but did not recall anyone with his distinctive traditional Chinese truth tattoo with Latin underneath or even any white people with Asian characters on their arm recently.

Billy then configured a complex string of search phrases to immediately alert him when anything even remotely related to Jacob's description, likely behaviour or mental distress was crawled by the news search bot. Something popped up about an Aboriginal knife but that was a red herring.

With all that cash, Jacob would be hard to trace but Cherry watched their bank account hourly and then logged into Jacob's ride share account by guessing the password. A ride share trip just showed up as in progress from Penrith to Watsons Bay on the opposite end of Sydney.

Penrith didn't seem significant except for the bird sanctuary there, but Watsons Bay was near Jacob's rich ex-girlfriend's house. It was also home to a cliff where many people jumped to their death called The Gap.

"Oh my God. The Gap" yelled Cherry as she reunited with Billy and Aroha from their search of the area. Aroha thought she had lost it and was exclaiming about a sale from the clothing store of the same name. Billy however immediately thought about the many people who had committed suicide by jumping off the cliffs of The Gap while also thinking about many gay men pushed to their death off cliffs around Sydney -especially in the late 1980s.

~ 15 ~

FIFTEEN

Cherry phoned Liverpool Police to report they were going to Watsons Bay.

"Take him to the nearest police if he is a danger" said the Liverpool officer.

"We can't come unless he is an immediate and severe danger to himself or others, call the hospital" said Rose Bay police near Watsons Bay.

"Take him to back to the hospital from the last admission" said the crisis team for the Eastern Suburbs.

"We would take him but don't have beds at the moment sorry, he can go to Liverpool maybe" said the Inner West team to Cherry who now replied with an unfamiliar tone of anger that also made it harder for her to think.

"If you bring him back to Liverpool, he will need the police" said the crisis team based only two blocks from their home.

It was like knocking on five government doors but all of them turning you away. They actually all had a 'no wrong door' policy obliging them to give practical help right away and assist with a handover to the right agency rather than flick people between each silo. Each agency was too constrained by time, geography and lack of knowledge on supporting carers or consumers in crisis.

It is tragically ironic that many do not get help when they ask for it but can get quickly hospitalised when they don't want it. For those who showed up to ED, police or crisis teams asking for help, they were often seen as too well to need a bed because they still had insight into their current mental state. Those who resisted help are seen as more likely to not understand how their mental state might damage their reputation, lead to accidents or escalate into violence. In a triage system with so few beds, the risks right now had to be prioritised over a more proactive prevention system.

Cherry felt like she was navigating a maze with only dead ends. Aroha seemed to have a bird's-eye view of parts of that maze, but he knew many of the exits still closed depending on what was going on there. He knew driving Jacob to the closest ED was the best option if they could get him there safely even though it might still mean more time in a locked ward.

It took just over an hour to drive across from Sydney's South West to the East. The little village of Watsons Bay might have attracted Jacob for a few reasons. He may have gone there for the bush walk around the peninsula, for a chilled reflective picnic with fish and chips on the bayside, a stair climb to The Gap lookout, or a meet up with the old fling who lived nearby at Vaucluse.

Jacob and Bich were only together a year but that was going back a decade or so now. Bich's Vietnamese-born father had schizophrenia and she had acute anxiety. It was a mutual breakup for Bich and Jacob and they had not stayed in touch so the idea that they might be meeting didn't make sense. Still, such a trip across town alone without telling anyone didn't make much sense.

The ride share had stopped on the harbour side of Watsons Bay 48 minutes before Cherry, Aroha and Billy arrived together. At least it wasn't along the Tasman Sea side of the suburb where The Gap was. The three split up in individual search parties again -one east, one west and one along the peninsula to the north.

Aroha was on north patrol and soon walked near Lady Bay Beach. Clothes are optional at this beach and he spotted a some-what muscular man with just a bit of fat curled into a foetal po-sition. He leapt down the stairs to the harbour beach and scared the naked man who was curled into that position to read a novel more comfortably. It was not Jacob. Aroha ran back to the track.

'No persons allowed outside this fence' read the sign at The Gap where Billy had now climbed. He took the eastern search to avoid Cherry potentially spotting her husband's corpse down below. Always with somewhat of a hero complex, Billy imagined himself as the next Don Ritchie who lived nearby and helped those contemplating suicide at the edge of The Gap. This Angel of The Gap had saved over 160 people from suicide but passed away eight years ago. Now we rely more on people taking the first step to save themselves by making a call to Life Callback.

No one around had seen anyone matching Jacob's description. There were no signs of anyone on the edge or near the crashing waves below.

Jacob might be OK, but the odds were stacked against this maths teacher. The rate of suicide is expected to increase by al-most 14% in next 5 years according to a 2020 report. Suicide rates will be even worse in a possible scenario if unemployment reaches rises significantly. For Jacob demographically and with his recent episodes, the odds were even less in his favour.

Cherry bumped into a little girl as she was constantly checking her phone for digital signatures showing her husband was still alive. She hurried around the western side of the bay and showed a photo of her and husband together asking as many people as possible to look out for him.

A child with a toy gun startled Cherry into thoughts of death or perhaps Jacob hurting others. He wasn't that type of person, but she wasn't sure she really knew her husband anymore and had no real idea of what his voices might be telling him. Had he made a Leilira blade for some reason?

She heard a car skid and then thought of the tragic massacre of six people and injury of many by a car rampage in Melbourne three years ago. Symptoms of schizophrenia were seen as a cause but surely Jacob wouldn't be homicidal.

Cherry was at least now well aware that people with schizophrenia do not have a split personality. Multiple personalities or Dissociative Identity Disorder are much rarer than schizophrenia and those conditions are much less sinister and random than many believe. Schizophrenia is not a personality or sudden change of identities. Still, false beliefs become social stigma tattooed on people with schizophrenia that can become internalised to affect a sense of identity. Jacob needed to reclaim parts of old identity and avoid listening to people that labelled him 'a schizophrenic' as if he was nothing more than his diagnosis.

There were so many people with symptoms of schizophrenia, but it only took a handful to tar everyone with the same brush. This was then amplified by Hollywood and sensationalist news. Real stories are rarely told because they are either too normal or hushed up because of shame combined with a valid fear of discrimination.

Cherry irrationally knocked on the accessible toilet to check if Jacob was there washing his face like his compulsive efforts to trigger the dive response during a night of acute delusions. Looking at the wheelchair symbol on the toilet door, Cherry started to see Jacob as having a disability. If Jacob had a wheelchair, people would be outraged if they witnessed such overt discrimination that Jacob had felt those last few months. At least his stigma was mostly invisible unlike psychical disabilities but even the way people throw around words like 'psycho', 'crazy' and 'mental breakdown' were jarring for Jacob.

Jacob could not be cured of schizophrenia, but medication and therapy still works for most people. Cherry just worried about many more possible wild goose chases if Jacob were to relapse again. She wondered whether he thought the same thing and had decided to end his life by failing to see that he could overcome symptoms or live well despite them.

Near one of the yacht clubs, Cherry noticed two men holding hands. Despite being such a gay city, it was still rare to see two men holding hands except around Oxford Street. The proud display of public affection would be an extremely brave act in her home suburb of Liverpool. Here in Watsons Bay it was less out of place but still reminded Cherry of the stigma and discrimination that the LGBTQI+ community faced and how hard the community fought to survive it or eliminate it. "It gets better!" remembered Cherry of the now decade-old slogan that still gave hope to that community and would become a positive mantra for Cherry.

Aroha and Billy hadn't texted yet, "no news is good news I hope" thought Cherry now concerned she would be the one to find her husband acting violently or a victim of his own self-harm. In fact, people with schizophrenia are much more likely to be victims of violence rather than perpetrators. Cherry was catastrophising and had failed to see that the precious heart of the old Jacob was still beating.

Finally, a sign of life, or perhaps theft of Jacob's credit card:

21 Nov 2020PENDING - Watsons Boutique Hotel AUS - $ 299.00

Cherry saw the date and realised she had forgotten it was the 21st. It was their five-year wedding anniversary. What a terribly panicked and worrying start to the milestone. Reflecting on the man she married in 2015 compared to how he acted this year, Cherry sobbed dramatically while sprinting along Marine Parade through the park, past the very busy fish and chips take away to the hotel. All those she passed heard her sob and just stared with no attempt to consul her or even say any quick word of reassurance as she raced past.

The hotel reception told her that her husband checked in early but wouldn't give a room number or key. She raced between rooms frantically knocking on each door and was tempted to steal a master key hanging from a maid's trolley. Instead, she asked politely if she could have one of the mini moisturiser bottles and used it to sooth herself through the gentle touch rubbing on her face as she noticed the pleasant smell.

She then had just enough of a window of clarity to think of her next move.

There were only 32 rooms with many now being cleaned before the 2pm check-in. She walked casually door-to-door and gently explained to anyone who answered that she was looking for her husband who had a big night and forgot to tell her which room he was in. They believed her and were mostly unbothered by her interruption.

As she went door-to-door she fondly remembered eight years ago to the day when Jacob sent a Facebook message after seeing Cherry post a funny meme in a shared group. She also remembered six years ago to the day when Jacob proposed and their beautiful wedding exactly five years ago. The alignment of all three anniversaries seemed mathematically pure but it was really crafted by Jacob to prevent him from having to remember so many dates!

Their wedding was by the water and she imagined the reflection of the reception on the bay below. The memory was now blurred because of the ongoing shockwaves of 2020. The memory of the wedding would last forever but waves of this year would still remain as ripples forever.

She got to room 14 which had its door slightly ajar. The 4 in the room number was a bad omen for Cherry as she had the slightest tetraphobia. Like many Mandarin-speaking people, she was somewhat afraid or superstitious of the number for linguistic and traditional reasons.

Cherry was shocked when she entered and saw the bed was covered in a deep red around an outline of a lifeless white creature in the centre.

~ 16 ~

SIXTEEN

The deep red of rose petals outlined the rough shape of a dove.

"Great! You solved the riddle faster than I expected. But we're not ready. I'm so sorry for the argument and for not coming home. I thought this grand gesture would be more interesting than breakfast in bed for our anniversary and for making you worry, and oh yeah, happy anniversary" blurted out Jacob knowing an even more awkward moment was on its way.

"It's OK, you're safe but why here and why'd you buy a platinum dating app subscription?" said Cherry concerned but still somewhat trusting.

"Look in your purse, there's a red envelope" said Jacob deflecting the dating app question for now. She pulled out a post-it from inside the red pocket (*hongbao*) that read mostly pictographically:

THE OLD JACOB = 14

The mix of icons, clipart and fonts Jacob liked was crudely cryptic but referred to a series of in-jokes or cultural references that gradually made sense to Cherry as:

> Go downstairs at 2pm for a ride share that will take you to Watsons Boutique Hotel where the old Jacob...

The 14 in a heart was still confusing – a reference to Valentine's Day as well as the room number?

"The 14 is like when I used to get *shí sì* for 14 mixed up with *shì sǐ* for 'is dead'! The old Jacob is still here but we still need to mourn the stability, certainty and parts of my identity that I lost in March" explained Jacob to his wife.

Cherry would have immediately seen the red pocket as soon as she bought her morning flat white but did not even take time for that small bit of self-care that frantic morning.

The couple had only briefly lost their love of cheeky riddles and games like this. Jacob had seized back this part of his old self and made a special effort, albeit a somewhat failed one, to celebrate their shared love of pleasant surprises. These were essential in a year of so many awful and tragic shocks for everyone.

The dove outlined in rose petals on the bed held a long-stem burgundy rose in its mouth. Jacob picked it up and offered it like an olive branch. The rose was such a dark red that it had a funerary quality which was overly macabre even with the planned mourning of lost aspects of self.

To lighten the mood, Jacob got out his phone and skipped ahead a bit on one track.

"I'm sorry, the old Taylor can't come to the phone right now"

"Why?"

"Oh, 'cause she's dead!"

The two laughed and cringed at the same time. Jacob chose the song because they sung it together at karaoke one time but also because their surname was often mistaken for Taylor.

Aroha and Billy arrived after getting the text message that everything was OK. As they entered Room 14 they were immediately taken aback by both the harbour views and the blaring Taylor Swift song. Cherry and Jacob carried on singing while in some kind of awkward but touching dance battle.

"Oh, look what you made me do!" the four chanted in unison.

A Vietnamese woman knocked on the door -perhaps a noise complaint. She was wheeling super expensive hand luggage.

"This is Bich" said Jacob which meant Jade in Vietnamese and was not pronounced like the swear word it seemed to be. "We used to date" explained Jacob as Bich nodded uncomfortably.

Bich and Cherry ran toward each other exchanging slaps with Cherry then grabbing Bich's white blouse which tore off the top three buttons or so at least that was what Billy incorrectly imagined.

In fact, Cherry wasn't the jealous type until the platinum dating app purchase and as Bich opened the designer bag, her reason for being there became clear. She was running errands to help Jacob buy:

1. Two chilled bottles of fine champagne
2. Handcrafted white chocolate honeycomb clusters
3. A selection of *pain au chocolat* and croissants
4. Sesame and cumin lavosh crackers
5. Beetroot and orange dip

These items were *so* Eastern Sydney but were also very Cherry.

"I used the dating app to track down Bich because she's not on social media. She helped me plan everything and drove to the Rose Bay shops. It would have been timed properly if you got the ride share, I ordered for 2 o'clock" Jacob explained. Bich was also a helpful ear because she had been there for her father to support his episodes of schizophrenia.

"Aww, maybe one of your voices is cupid" joked Cherry. Too soon.

With the romantic setting and now nice food and drinks, the others left the couple to relax and have a much-needed nap in the luxurious king bed.

Awaking to an alarm of a playlist called 'Coastal Chill', the married couple reflected on the frantic search around Sydney. Jacob listened carefully to the rhythm, tempo and lyrics of the playlist to self-soothe back closer to reality. Half of a PRN pill also helped him from flying off the rails that night but made the champagne a bit stronger than normal, and not in a good way.

They were both a bit tipsy at dinner with Jacob leaving the fishier parts of their multi-layered seafood basket to his wife. Having just a small bit of alcohol seemed like a good way to pardon his ongoing unusual observations and interactions with the waiters. Too much might interact badly with the medication or lead Jacob to drink more as each sip lowered his inhibitions and gave him a little rush that he wanted more of.

It was a nice night -practically uneventful compared to the drama before finding Jacob. The booze was tolerated enough for them both to have fun but still be happy for an early night. It was a bit more boring than might be expected of an anniversary evening but that was OK with both of them for now.

Cherry rushed back home in the early hours of the next day leaving Jacob to sleep-in until check out. She put on her best pinstripe pant suit and decided that the old Cherry was dead too. She imagined herself like the paralegal in her favourite show who then started at a prestigious law school and became partner in a corporate firm but with a social justice spin. She found passion and motivation in picturing herself taking on many *pro bono* cases for those incarcerated under the *Mental Health Act* and their carers.

On the 31st floor of the reopened law firm, Cherry used her break to enrol in law school at one of the top schools in Sydney. Class would blend online and face-to-face because Covid had changed their delivery model. Luckily this provided more flexibility for a full-time worker like Cherry but still gave her much-needed alumni networks forged in real life classes.

The key to her success in this postgrad *Juris Doctor* degree was to apply as many assignments as possible to her work and hypotheticals of future health law cases she might take. Jacob could provide a sounding board and help her remain grounded so she could eventually explain the law to her clients who also had ongoing symptoms of mental distress.

Jacob took it easy most days in the fortnight following his Watsons Bay visit. The weather waivered from intense heat slowing his work down to rain discouraging him from going for walks. Fortunately, the heat made him rest more and not work too hard on getting Well Tree back online.

Aroha came and visited every few days to make sure his mate had something useful and interesting to do. Though their conversations were unlike the emotion-sharing and deep listening Aroha had with Billy, the purposeful activities they did together were still highly therapeutic. They built a raised garden bed out of wood that could move gently on recycled office chair wheels along the balcony railing of the Liverpool apartment. This would help avoid the intense sun and also move to where the rain was or out of the way when Jacob wanted to look out to the sunset.

Jacob's simple acts of making something from raw materials was meaningful and showed tangible progress toward the betterment of his life and the home he shared with his wife.

The next day's project was a bird feeder to hopefully attract some native lorikeets or cockatoos. The feeder looked like a wooden pavilion and the seed bell hanging from it attracted the occasional wild bird. A magpie perched on the feeder the next day but seemed to want meat rather than seed.

As Jacob stared down to his still-growing belly he thought it best not to feed the magpie anything too unhealthy. Looking up what magpies eat, he noticed that raw meat might infect them with the *Toxoplasma gondii* parasite. *T. gondii* was common in cat poo and found to be a potential cause of toxoplasmosis leading to schizophrenia. As Jacob stumbled on the string of related science mag articles on the topic, he read:

> "*T. gondii* might rewire a human brain permanently like it has in mice with the parasite. Many of these mice are now irrationally unafraid of cats... A study of 200 people in New Zealander with *T. gondii* didn't have much higher odds of schizophrenia... but at certain stages of

life the parasite may eventually waken an existing pre-disposition to mental illness."

Rather than blame his childhood cat, Jacob found the evidence just another reminder of how much we didn't know about biological and environmental causes of psychotic illnesses like schizophrenia. Now that knowledge of this parasite's link to schizophrenia was becoming well known, would people stop getting cats or even put their cats up for adoption or euthanasia?

The silly thought of cats, their poo and the parasites inside was so ridiculous that it made Jacob more comfortable about sharing his genes with his future children. Asian genes tended to be more dominant in many ways for whatever reason, perhaps that might change the probabilities even further.

He then used his university alumni journal subscriptions to read about teens who smoked dope being much more likely to get schizophrenia. This was only during a certain age though and may have been an association rather than causation with the actual cause of psychosis being something unknown. Below average birthweight could have caused a predisposition to depression causing psychosis directly but also being associated with a greater interest in escapism causing more use of drugs. The many combinations and permutations of causal chains like this quickly tired Jacob despite being satisfyingly quantifiable.

Biomarkers and genes that we can't yet identify or count might be much more reliable. Still, the brain was not an organ of chemicals and firing neurons, there was something beyond biology that we will never be smart enough to fully understand.

Causes of psychosis are such a constellation of so many unknowns that Jacob knew Well Tree must contribute somehow to mental health research as well as practice.

Jacob also started to look at non-medical explanations for his recent experiences. The Hearing Voices Network focused on voices or visions as occurring because of experiences like trauma rather than just chemicals or genes. Sensing something that others cannot see might be spiritual, paranormal, a special gift, a reaction to emotional distress, or a cognitive error. These options provided Jacob with more questions especially – could psychiatry be completely wrong here?

Schizophrenia itself was just a label for a set of experiences and is now often considered along a spectrum but with greyed out and sometimes blurred sections rather than clear points along a scale. Jacob might be on some mild end of this spectrum or on the rare and extreme far right section prone to violence.

The schizophrenia spectrum is not as convenient to categorise as something like the left-right political spectrum. The far right in US politics were becoming more vocal and potentially violent triggered by the elections which might foreshadow Jacob's possible extreme behaviour in the coming weeks.

There were no answers to these questions right now, but Jacob started to learn what to do to minimise his chances of relapse or at least recognise signs he was headed there. This takes considerable time and due to the common problem of anosognosia -a lack of insight into your own symptoms, Jacob's wife, friends and mum would need to be trained to also watch for warning signs.

As an image to be shared in everyone's mind, a simple traffic light system was all that was needed. Green meant everything was good to go and there were no out-of-character behaviours or unusual observations except for new realisations grounded in logic and evidence. Amber was a sign to slow down and prepare to stop. If Jacob did not stop, there was a strong chance of an accident when showing amber warning signs of less sleep, more distraction due to louder voices, and suspiciousness of people, coincidences or birds.

It was OK to still have new ideas that didn't meet norms but when they were well outside Aboriginal, Anglo-Australian or even Taiwanese frames, self-care and extra medication would be recommended to Jacob. If he refused or made threats, this would be a red light and immediate calls for help and hospitalisation would have to follow.

It was difficult for Jacob to accept that he might need to go back to hospital. He would make special efforts to catch a relapse early while learning that even the most terrible wards are better alternatives to roaming the streets while very unwell. Again, due to possible anosognosia, Jacob would also learn to accept that he may be forced to hospital by police or others if he stopped questioning delusions or started acting on what his voices commanded him to do.

~ 17 ~

SEVENTEEN

Billy got out Christmas decorations while playing remixed Christmas carols. His cat Y playfully chased the LED lights as he strung them up the loft stairs. Weaving around the top stairs, Billy climbed around the outside of the mezzanine railing to attach them to so they could hang up the wall and illuminate the pansexual flag.

Losing balance slightly as he tried to reach the timber flag frame, Billy fell the three metres to the wooden floor. He was having a seizure. There was no one around to see the loss of consciousness and convulsions.

The seizure lasted about a minute a half but no one was there to witness it except his cat who made a loud low-pitch cry as it happened. Y was again reacting to Billy's mood and behaviour but unfortunately her cries were unheard by neighbours through the brick walls.

Billy never had a seizure before but was on anti-seizure meds because they also treated mood disorders like bipolar. When he regained consciousness, he felt confused but also had a sense of *déjà vu*. His sore tongue and wet patch on his tracksuit pants reminded him of a doco on grand mal seizures which he was now known as a tonic-clonic seizure.

Seizures have also been found to be caused by Covid infection.

When trying to get fresh pants on, Billy realised how painful it was to lift his left leg. Something was definitely broken. He put on a face mask and limped out the hall where his neighbour Ted was just leaving the house.

Billy and Ted had not become friends but had many things in common despite Billy's fear when his neighbour came into their building in police uniform one time. It was not that Billy was a criminal but the experience being cornered and taken to hospital by police was embarrassing on a good day and traumatising most others. This was interlaced with memories of uniformed security guards who were heavy-handed in the hospital.

Ted could see Billy was injured and offered to take him to the hospital. "It will be Bill and Ted's Bogus Journey" said the dorky copper. "Party on dude" Billy groaned as the two walked to Ted's car.

The broken bone or two meant an X-ray would be needed but Billy was desperate to avoid ED in case they saw his record in the psych ward and decided to lock him up again. It was awful to have this place of healing where lives are saved tainted by fears of Covid infection and then have the psych ward experience intensify the reluctance to get help when was clearly needed.

Having helped hospitals schedule many patients before, Ted encouraged Billy to go with him to a different ED than the one he went to that year. The different environment would be less likely to trigger a bad memory. The two hospitals would take a similar amount of time because of traffic even though one was within the district boundaries of their lofts. Ambulances in Sydney must take you to the closest ED available so the choice of two hospitals here was a luxury.

The added benefit of changing districts was that there was still very little data exchange between them. This artificially divided sections of the same public health system. Their software was different and couldn't handover the psych records automatically. So, to the new hospital, Billy did not appear to have any mental health issues. A set of bureaucratic and technological failures protected Billy from being seen as 'mental' but also presented many dangers to other patients whose pre-existing and past injuries might be missed unless they were understood and shared by a conscious patient or eventually shared and re-entered to the new district's medical record. Ridiculously, a faxed copy of a hand-written paper file would have been more advanced and would expedite the situation here.

Having Ted take time to comfort him and deeply listen to his physical and emotional pain made Billy re-think his attitude toward police. Maybe it wasn't that All Cops Are Bastards (ACAB) but just Most Cops A Bastards (MCAB) – a small but important improvement in the year of BLM. Rather than share his new acronym Billy paraphrased a police PR campaign by gently saying "maybe some cops are tops" to his new mate.

The health screening at ED had become lax and there were not many other patients in triage. With a quick examination, pain medication and fitting of a leg brace, the X-ray could be done later. The seizure was put down to the fall rather than a sign of epilepsy, but it was still unclear whether the seizure might have caused the fall in the first place or consciousness was only lost after the impact.

The use of anti-epileptic drugs for mood disorders intrigued Billy. The physical shockwaves of a seizure were somehow a strange parallel to both the emotional shockwaves after a major stressor. The shockwaves continued like tremors in his hands that were still medication side effects.

Luckily, Billy had built up a few more sick days so could have a few days off. Rather than rest up, he turned back to Well Tree. The comparisons to a physical injury and the leg brace used to protect usual walking around from aggravating the injury helped Billy to sketch out the first major branches of the app.

"Start with Y" thought Billy as his fingers ran through his darling cat's soft long fur. He was recalling a talk on the web about the need to start asking 'Why?' before any decisions are made or strategies developed. The 'Why?' here was the overall vision of mending holes in the fabric of society to improve well-being. The vexing issues of homelessness, mental illness and physical health were the key holes that needed interwoven mending.

Reorienting his life and the Well Tree venture to be about being a master tailor repairing worn and broken sections of society made more sense than just launching an app. Overloaded with metaphors, he imagined himself not as a tailor fixing what was broken but as a gardener creating fertile environments for Well Tree to grow organically. It was still a sapling nurtured well by Jacob with help from Cherry but now they had to reorient back to regrowing their own lives again so Cherry would be ready for work and study next year.

At work, Billy was tweaking one of their form builder tools used mostly for surveys or marketing subscriptions. He realised if he used this free tool, there wouldn't be much coding at all as there was a simple engine for making decision trees based on form responses.

What this meant in lay terms was a faster way to capture what was going well, what was going wrong and what needed to change in the lives of those using the app. If there was a crisis, the problem would need to be quickly detected and the right help found immediately.

"Some hardcoding or a plugin would easily use the geolocation, time and date to find the right help for that time and place" thought Billy while geeking-out to his new idea.

Looking at an app with a similar goal, there were over 70 questions before any advice was offered -a barrier much too high for most.

Rapid prototyping of alternate models and then testing them on his friends' actual symptoms was possible because the main features were already there and free to adapt to this unique use-case.

Each leaf of the tree could be colour-coded with overall data then colouring the tree with reds and ambers for autumn or green in spring and watching for the changes between seasons. Like Jacob's principles of gamification, the greener trees could be rewarded with leaf badges for practicing skills or self-care.

He then compared the situation of having no leave in hospital to a tree with no leaves -able to survive for a while but would then wither and die.

Billy realised this needed to be an app more about preventing a crisis rather than just reacting to it. The first prototype came together as a simple hierarchy of:

Billy used the Black Friday sale to reward himself for his recent colourful creation. If only his two new 2021 dancing and singing games synced up somehow so he could do both his self-soothing activity of singing and fun cardio at the same time. He hooked up a lapel mic to a speaker while playing the dancing game and his amplified laughter at the ridiculousness of this solo activity echoed up the loft.

In his shopping, Billy also made the seemingly random purchase of quilting materials. He planned to make a Japanese-style quillow - a quilt that folded like origami into a pillow. Along with nine fabric squares like a rainbow of kimonos, he purchased satin letters that would read QUILTBAG as well as a small + symbol.

Very carefully Billy hand-sewed the nine cotton squares and back pouch to make the pillow part. The clashing patchwork of textiles was sewn together with a deliberately thick and noticeable purple quilting thread. It was a Christmas gift to thank his parents for helping him get through the difficult year but also a way to come out of the closet to them.

Henry and Joy would need a basic explanation of the diverse range of sexual orientations, gender identities and gender expressions.

Billy would later explain it as a QUILTBAG quilt. The acronym was an easier way to spell out the alphabet soup of an expanding and diverse community. Queer, Undecided, Intersex, Lesbian, Trans, Bisexual, Asexual, Gay and a + for many other communities like those who are pansexual.

It wasn't about gay and lesbian rights anymore; it was much more inclusive. Likewise, the progress made by advocates for treatment and research for those experiencing depression and anxiety needed to become more inclusive to those with less common but more complex conditions.

He hadn't even included a P for Pansexual in the quilt but the idea that pan could be attraction to anyone meant that the quilt covered him nicely anyway. His parents would definitely think he was gay though with that level of talent in textiles combining with their existing suspicions.

Many years later some of the patches faded and the lighter areas changed colour slightly after a few washes as if the boundaries of each square were not so clear-cut. What remained though was the thick purple thread bringing the patch-work together as one strong and comforting whole.

The 'Mad Pride' movement had borrowed principles of 'coming out proud' from the gay and lesbian rights movement. Billy was not actually proud of his mental scars but would share the story of how they got there. His bruises from the fall faded like some of his bad memories but the scars remained.

Billy used his wrong turns and reflections on the diverse experiences likely for people with mental distress to work on the app again. He included in each prototype as many possible branches of the Well Tree as was practical without needing to ask too many questions of app users.

He then thought about how he might get people to install the app or use the mobile web version. There was a way to target ads to the specific keywords and cookie history of past websites accessed. This level of stalking didn't sit well with Billy even though the ends seemed to justify the means. He was a White Hat hacker meaning he used his ability to crack systems in order to help others but tracking mental distress seemed a bit too Grey Hat.

Back at work a few days later, the somewhat socially distanced Christmas party led to concerns about his leg brace. No one had really asked about his leave while they were mostly working from home, but the visible injury was a conversation starter bringing empathy from those who had experienced a broken bone before.

After a few too many refills of the alcoholic rhubarb, pomegranate and kombucha punch, Billy decided he would come out of the closet.

"This broken bone was not nearly as bad as my mental breakdown this year" he said to a group of three team members which was met with awkward silence. He then cleverly flipped the narrative to share how he was using their forms engine to help others in mental distress. Ideas started flowing on sub-branches of the tree with many sharing details of distress they or someone they knew experienced.

With an estimated one in five Australians affected by complex mental illness, it was not just everyday nervousness, stress or feeling sad but chronic conditions being shared. Despite the open culture and apparent commitment to staff wellbeing, these topics were unsafe to share at the Christmas party. Alcohol led to oversharing personal details and sharing of others' stories without their permission or any attempt to deidentify them.

Others tried to use their experiences in lockdown to try to relate to the distress Billy had felt. Everyone felt different stressors differently but this attempt to empathise was insulting. A locked ward is nothing like a nice home you can still leave often under certain conditions.

Still, Billy was happy to be out with his symptoms and seemed to have avoided Jessie's main problem of disclosure because he went through official channels to confirm he was OK to work. If they fired him now, they would have to use some other way to justify it and even then, could be sued under anti-discrimination laws or smeared by bad PR -something this company was very concerned with.

Word spread quickly through the harbour party venue about Billy's admission. He noticed some stares so thought of ways to reassure everyone that right now he was totally 'all-right'. A very senior manager mingled his way gradually toward Billy who now thought he was in trouble.

"Sounds like you're using Forms in ways that might get us some good press" said Shel. "Tell me more now and maybe you can pitch it to the social responsibility team on Friday" she offered.

The camera in Billy's phone activated. A background app was tracking his location and occasionally recorded his face and his voice.

~ 18 ~

EIGHTEEN

Jessie came up from Canberra on Thursday morning and met Jacob and Billy to help with the Well Tree corporate pitch. She would bring flair, energy and excitement to the pitch like she did with events she planned.

Jacob covered the financials under the assumption that he must know about accounting and securing funds because he was good at maths. Luckily, Billy had worked on enough projects to use budgeting software and ge understood the basics of building a business case for internal funds for a new app.

It was rare to have working prototypes for a first pitch, but a link was shared so each of the social responsibility execs could see the mobile-optimised website on their own phone or tablet. They could see it was their form engine and entered dummy data to answer some of the form questions. The conference room projector also shared the screen with an exec in the Texas office displayed a beautiful 3D tree changing colours with their responses in real-time. It was a nice change from the usual 'death by slides' they were used to.

Jessie came along to live-draw the very positive feedback from the execs on a smartboard so it could be shared with Texas and used by the team later.

It all looked like a positive way to improve mental health but the execs were worried with how much money it would need and what the company would get out of it.

The request was a $495K seed grant, paid time for 4 coders and 2 designers from the company to spend 4 weeks on the pilot app, and office space for three years. It was a bit more than a modest investment but was not just corporate philanthropy. The venture would demonstrate how dynamic the company's forms engine could be.

The return on investment might be considerable given that there would also be a research arm bringing in university partners for funding. This research could improve form functionality, embed AI into forms so they branch out more effectively which would help make their whole form engine much more useful. Additional research could also evaluate of how effective each skill, helpline or treatment option was at turning leaves from red to amber to green.

The most exciting part of the pitch for these tech execs who were almost all past or current gamers was the gamification mechanics. As the interest of the execs peaked, Billy's face stopped being as warm as before. XP would be earned by users for doing healthy daily activities to level up as they would be more likely to prevent illness and be better prepared for distress when it came. Badges would be issued for turning your own leaf from red to amber or amber to green or helping someone else upgrade their leaves in this way.

"Could it have a leaderboard for the tree with the most green leaves?" said a senior exec with a Type A personality.

"We thought of that but we now think it's OK to have leaves of many colours as long as the whole tree is healthy and stable" said Jacob even though he did like the idea of quantifying wellness somehow. "Yes, like saying: 'It's OK not to be OK'!" explained Jessie whose brown leaves had started to gently drop off the tree in her beta version of the app – a feature which she designed.

"We still have a lease on The Factory but no longer need it as the hotdesks here are now enough with more people working from home" said Shel who popped in for the last part of the pitch meeting. As the offer came Billy could barely hold in his laughter. Jacob and Jessie did not realise that they were just being handed a space called The Factory with fit-out for 88 desks and 4 meeting rooms under a ceiling that vaulted up 12 metres.

They joined Aroha to open their new office with the oversized metal key. The giant wooden doors seemed out of place for a tech firm. Distressed brick walls, heritage columns, and polished concrete floors were overwhelmingly exciting and matched the kind of style Billy had crafted in his loft but on a grand scale. The metal trusses 10 metres up were used to hang retractable power and ethernet cables to the desks and printers that were left for them along with dust and a few rats.

The giant industrial ceiling fans kept the place pretty cool even with its many sky lights bringing the summer sun inside. There was also infrared strip heating along some of the trusses that would mean a considerable budget overrun just on power bills during winter.

Committing to the $1 three-year lease with Billy's employer now meant actually delivering something. The prototypes looked great but rolling them out would take a lot of effort because an app not evidence-based and untested with a pilot could offer inappropriate advice to people who really need help.

The enormity of their 'nice problem to have' quickly sunk in. They met at a nearby bar to brainstorm how they might use the space. The bar was at the confluence of three urban canals and was similar to the new office in terms of converting an old warehouse into a bohemian commercial space.

"We definitely need a massive native tree in the centre with seating all around" offered Jessie while realising that this would only superficially fill such a big space. She felt like they were being wasteful in taking a large space even though so many shops had closed permanently, and skyscrapers were still more than half empty. The new hub for the next three years was surrounded by three largely empty corporate towers that were like barren mountains surrounding their peaked-roof warehouse.

"We can get some youthful energy and ideas from summer interns from the two unis nearby" she suggested. Hordes of programming, design and marketing students could easily be given internships -especially among the international students who could not go back to their home countries for the holidays. She soon used some of her contacts from work at AAA to find the better students and made sure the team paid them enough of a wage so they wouldn't stress so much about covering rent. Rent stress had plagued international students in Sydney even in the early months of the pandemic and many had not been eating properly or buying the textbooks they needed.

Billy matched each student with one of the six mentors who joined from his company and as Jacob worked well with young people as a teacher, he designed interesting training tracked along a large game board on the main wall. Billy picked two of the most promising coders for himself -now less of a mentee to Jessie or Aroha and more of a mentor to these students who had their own lived experience of chronic mental illness.

One of Billy's colleagues who volunteered to take the paid secondment to Well Tree was Allie who had worked closely with Billie. Al could see that Billy had changed a lot that year -mostly for the better but had still lost some of his spark. That spark was still beneath the surface somewhere or potentially replaced with a new set of passions that would motivate less of a focus on do things that just felt good to running this venture that helped himself, others and the greater good.

From one of the steel trusses, flags hung to represent the cultures and sub-cultures of each intern, volunteer or co-founder. Billy made sure to have a symbolically thick gold velvet rope bring all these flags together in a supportive tie. New partnerships, resources, skills and ideas were hung as large gift tags among tinsel on the 5-metre-tall native tree in the centre of the office housed in rusted metal bent into a cylinder.

Aroha had helped with the fit out and was often up 10 metres on the top rung of a ladder. He noticed that the cords could all be moved so that the space could be reconfigured easily. He assumed Jessie could think of ways to use the venue as an event space that could host a lot of people even with the ongoing need for distancing.

The events could teach carers, mental health consumers, clinicians and the community about what it's really like to go through a mental health crisis, what to do and more importantly -how to avoid it in the first place. It would be part of the Well Tree mission to run the training in the space and online but also learn from the individual participants' experiences to improve the app.

A revenue stream could be secured through a corporate training arm focusing on staff wellbeing which could subsidise other training or the app itself. With enough people doing the subsidised training, they would also have a large database of potential users of the app.

As well as the events idea, Jessie had two more innovative ideas for the flexible space. A modular system could create small rooms to box off all the desks on wheels, screens and printers in a corner protected from dust with a sheet of clear acrylic plastic glass. As she drew the idea on a whiteboard while looking up at the beams, columns and trusses, Jacob came over with curiosity.

"You want to turn the office into a bunch of fishbowls like the nurse stations?" asked Jacob.

It was like that with a focus on reducing noise, bring in natural light through the layer of acrylic sitting on the trusses but then moving everything back for office hours or evening events.

They would need more money for this experiment and Jessie suggested two unlikely sources: the health department and the housing department. The space could be the nexus of Jessie's three main passions: running events, helping the homeless, and reducing mental distress. The combination of clear and non-transparent coloured panels could create pods for when Well Tree programmers needed their own space to focus on coding during the day, could be moved for training and social support events at night, and become safe sleeping spaces for homeless people from 9pm-7am.

This kind of creative, ambitious and 'save the world' vision may have been a sign that Jessie was having grandiose delusions. The practicalities of keeping such a hybrid space clean and secure with each transition managed carefully were a bit too bold for the young social venture but started to get Jessie writing about her modern day Western Lapland and how it might mend the related holes in the fabric of society: homelessness, mental distress and access to education.

The vision could not be fulfilled yet as it would extend the Well Tree mission way too much for now, but Jessie predicted her eventual return as she followed one of the three nearby canals toward Central station. There were a lot more young people sleeping rough around canals and the railway tracks. Even in suburbs with nicer houses there were bags and cardboard used as uncomfortable sleeping mats. There were few places with air conditioning that would let these people stay for very long -certainly not to sleep. About 5,000 homeless people stayed in the inner city and there was nowhere near enough services for them. They were still at risk of Covid-infection but at much greater risk of developing chronic illness and being victims of violence.

Jessie wanted to save every one of them but still had some work to do to make her own Well Tree visualisation healthy and green enough so she could get badges helping others. Billy was already like a bowerbird collecting badges for his own self-care and collecting badges issued to him by the interns as they used the beta app to improve their own lives.

On her coach back to Canberra she planned the next WWW bushwalk. She would have everyone use the beta app before and after the walk to measure if the mindful walking strategies she shared had any impact on mood and intentions to do more wellness activities. Changing attitudes to illness and wellness must be followed up with changes to intentions. Then actual new behaviours must form into habits. It was like she was charting paths for the women in the group, but they had to regularly follow them to prevent the kinds of distress she had experienced and react better to distressful events out of their control.

One of the women in the group named Maya was very interested in Jessie's approaches. Maya was so impressed with Jessie's ability to regularly book out with her maximum of 20 paying attendees. Maya wondered whether she could incorporate the kinds of wellness check-ins and sensory activities into the domestic group travel experiences she had started promoting when her travel agency shut down in late March.

"I have a few group walks coming up that need interesting guides like you" said Maya to Jessie who was still out of work but not paying rent for the granny flat. "It might also lead to international tour guiding when flights come back" continued Maya. Jessie was very keen to explore the idea and even started to proactively plan promotional events for the current local trips and future international trips. These could start in New Zealand and then branch up to the Asia-Pacific with a local translator when needed to plan and negotiate.

Jessie had always admired her grandfather, now passed, who was a successful travel agent. While her dad's parents how somehow spawned a super villain, her mother's parents were caring role models. They lived a few suburbs away in Blackheath and occasionally rescued Jessie and her brother Sam from violent nights at their home in Katoomba.

After shadowing Maya on the first trip to the coast near Jervis Bay, Jessie was invited to plan and run a three-day hike. She was still quite chubby, and the second day of hills would be challenging but she seized the offer to guide 16 people from Katoomba to Jenolan Caves.

Getting to Katoomba a day early for planning brought back some terrifying memories which interrupted the occasionally pleasant nostalgia. At least Sam knew what it was like for Jessie growing up but the two did not dare talk about the family violence of the past when they met at the local pub that night.

With space in her tent and a need for a Plan B in case she was too unfit, Jessie asked if Sam wanted to come on the bushwalk.

Sam's violent outbursts had led him to have several apprehended violence orders (AVOs) against him to protect his victims. Jessie did not want to believe he had become like their father because he was still so kind to her.

Sam was on government payments like Jessie still and only had occasional gigs like she did. He did not have any work that week, so he braved the summer heat and overcame some of his social anxiety to interact with the 16 wealthy walkers paying for Jessie's salary and his food for the trip.

Sam dragged Jessie out of the tent on the first night of the hike to unroll their swags and sleep under the stars. Sam had escaped the probabilities of getting a psychotic illness, but his social anxiety could still be crippling, and his trauma led him to lash out -no excuse still. With the gentle sound of the flowing Megalong Creek nearby, the two started to speak openly about their father and the effect he had on their lives.

That night she luckily did not have any nightmares from her childhood. Instead, she dreamed of the Northern Lights over the top of The Factory that had randomly had snow on it and an Osprey perched on the unused chimney.

~ 19 ~

NINETEEN

Billy's mood swung like a pendulum from one end of sadness to the other end of energetic agitation. Sometimes these swings happened so quickly that it was like all emotions were blurred together. It wasn't that he had the kind of mood swings that people see as a fault of personality, it was inner experiences that he did not always outwardly express.

The big and slow swings were the worst but were closely followed by times when the pendulum barely swung at all -an absence of emotion. It was not like the rollercoaster of emotions experienced early that year. The flatness of this mood score of 5 felt like stagnant waters again with the stench of stalled progress like the odour of decomposing blue-green algae on a billabong that was once a nicely flowing river.

At least with the pendulum, there might be some more regularity and predictability but, in this case, there appeared to be some other disruptive force pulling and pushing him. The movement was unpredictably fast sometimes but at other times it restricted him to flatly not swing at all.

The sessions with Dr Lowenstein and his new psychologist were starting to help with skills, resources and therapies being fed back into Well Tree. It was like the sessions returned an investment for Billy personally and for his socially minded new venture. This thought made Billy feel he was more business-minded than he imagined which he was not completely proud of.

Work was flexible with Billy's hours over summer with the ability to work from home, from The Factory or from Pyrmont HQ. The change in scenery was nice but he decided to stick to set days in each location to get into a routine. Though they were doing good work at Well Tree, they wouldn't see clear results for a while and Billy needed something else in his weekly schedule to give him energy and purpose.

Aroha suggested church. Always a highly Christian man but rarely evangelical, Aroha had found purpose in his faith and belonging in his church community. His past mental distress was seen as a test from God which just sounded ridiculous to Billy when considering how cruel such a test was and how it led so many people to their deaths.

"God will not test you more than you can handle" proselytised Aroha. Billy used a Bible app on the way to a church that was closer to Billy's loft than Aroha's house in the West. He used the theme searching tool to look for references to Aroha's advice. Christians who Billy knew in the past tended to adapt the Bible's message in inappropriate ways to try to popularise it. The app gave a related snippet:

1 Corinthians 10:13

> "No testing will overtake you unless it is common to everyone. God is faithful, and he will not test you beyond your strength, but with the testing He will also provide the way out so that you may be able to endure it."

"Warning, warning, this is not a test Aroha, this is real life and God either doesn't exist or hates me!" said Billy followed with the more serious noting that, "I don't want to just endure life and survive, I want to thrive" said Billy as Aroha pointed to the sign in front of the church that showed the sermon theme today was 'THRIVE'!

A Christian believing in interventionist signs from God or perhaps people with religious delusions would have given a divine attribution to the unlikely link between Billy's statement and the literal church sign.

Billy thought in a more scientific way though. He thought he and the church minister were just on the same wavelength and had both watched a recently uploaded talk titled with the 'thrive not survive' cliché.

The church was from a less conservative faction than Aroha's church and the minister politely asked, "whether you are friends or a couple, you are very welcome here". Billy and Aroha were both comfortable to neither confirm or deny Reverend Patton's assumptions and jokingly grasped hands to test the minister's resolve.

A large tree in front of the church was as high as its spire. There were three high rise apartment buildings surrounding the church making the scene resemble The Factory slightly.

Walking through the large wooden doors Billy felt a sudden coldness and a disconnect between him and a higher power. Something that had been built to celebrate and understand God seemed to be a barrier between Billy and the universe. Though the congregation were friendly and tolerant, Billy could not forgive all the historical murder, guilt and shame created by Christendom in God's name.

During the sermon on thriving through faith, Billy noticed his arms were crossed. His body language showed he was no longer open to being converted to a new faith. His memories of school sermons came back. He couldn't understand how a school with such a vicious culture of bullying by staff and students could call itself Christian.

How could God allow so much pain in the world? Did He do this to make the world's beauty even more beautiful by comparison?

The Buddhist principles that superficially guided his interior decorating also spiritually guided Cherry and seemed a bit more useful as an explanation of mental illness. Shared with Hinduism, the Buddhist idea of *Duḥkha* couldn't be translated into one English word. *Duḥkha* is a sense of emptiness combined with experiences of suffering, unhappiness, pain, or stress. In Chinese *Duhkha* could be translated as ? meaning bitter which was an appropriate description of how Billy felt when his mood pendulum didn't swing.

The Buddhist idea that all existence involves suffering did not give much hope to Billy. He wondered whether a hopefulness for the second coming of Christ might actually be more useful -even if it might not be true. Reorienting away from his own beliefs to a respect for the beliefs of others, Billy wondered whether Well Tree could ask brief questions about culture or religion to give more appropriate techniques and treatment options.

Some medications are starting to become personalised to the genes, proteins, family history and past medical events. With psychosocial diseases, a more culturally grounded approach might also allow for personalised approaches to treatment. Telehealth could now match therapists more closely with linguistic, cultural, and sub-cultural profiles such as really specific matching of Billy with a Western-born Chinese male who is also attracted to more than one gender. With location less of an issue, matching very diverse characteristics were possible given the much larger pool of therapists.

Perhaps finding the right religion and then church community within it was also a complex matching process. It was clear that this particular church as not right for Billy, but he was still thankful for Aroha's efforts.

At the end of the service after the stale biscuits, Billy carefully explained to Aroha that he wanted to have faith but just couldn't -at least not after all the events of this year. He would have faith in his own abilities and draw strength from inside himself but still be open to learning about a higher power and how it might intervene in the lives of human beings.

He had similar conversations with the hospital chaplain who was spread too thin across the health district but was someone interesting to talk to when he was available. The chaplain would often come to visit Aino -the woman the trio called the Osprey.

Billy found the chaplain's email on a Christian directory website. He emailed to ask about the Osprey while also updating the chaplain on progress with Well Tree. As he was not employed by the hospital, there was a bit more scope to share information, but he still had legal and moral obligations to respect privacy. He decided it was the morally right thing to do to share a news article in the reply email along with a link on dealing with grief. The news article was dated December 1, 2020 and the main snippets read:

Hospital psych patient dies after struggle with security

A mentally ill patient reportedly became agitated on Sunday and screamed at nurses on the psychiatric ward she was held in for the past nine months. Internal sources in the hospital stated that the Finnish citizen wanted her cigarettes and wanted to go home and see her children again. She then allegedly assaulted a security guard who was trying to restrain her for an injection.

The struggle to the ground and resisting of the restraint led to a head injury with lengthy resuscitation efforts failing to save the 38-year-old.

The sufferer of psychotic depression had her deportation planned as soon as she was well enough to fly but now her husband and children will not see her alive again. Her body will be repatriated as soon as flights are available.

Sadness, anger and disbelief all filled Billy's mind as he read each line. He was devastated for the grieving family, angry at the hospital and it's security guards while also not believing that this slim and melancholic Christian woman had attacked anyone. Perhaps a Big Brother situation of constant surveillance would have been preferable to the family never really knowing how the lost soul they loved ended up leaving this world before reaching 40.

Billy ignored the self-care strategies of the grief article in the second link as he felt he didn't know this woman well. He was intensely sad for Aino and her family, but the real shock was that something similar could have happened to him or his friends. Billy messaged Jessie as he remembered that her and Aino had a moment together at least once.

The Osprey named Aino was caged like all of Billy's former fellow patients. For Billy, the short stay was enough to change him forever, but nothing compared to Aino's nine months without leaving the 240m^2 ward. A feeling of institutionalisation set in for Aino on three fronts: imitating routines so much there would be a total sense of dependence on discharge, losing all trust in fairness of the law, complying with norms of the ward and, striving for 'normal' with no ambitious goals.

Aino's husband, 9-year-old son and 5-year-old daughter had their trip to join her postponed by Covid. The kids would not be allowed to visit her under the changed visitation policies of the hospital in any case. She stayed alive for them but then fought so hard to get out that she was fatally injured in the process. Christmas in a few weeks would be very tough and the empty chair at the Christmas table would be an annual reminder of the tragedy.

As the weather in Finland went to sub-zero, Sydney reached 42°C. Finland's Covid deaths were still quite low but cases were climbing over the last few months in contrast to three weeks of zero cases in Sydney. Despite the Finnish openness about mental illness, Aino's family would not share the details of her death with their community. Death by SARS-CoV-2 which is the disease caused by COVID-19 would have been a longer death but Aino's death must have still be painful and unlike Covid, carried stigma and shame with an even greater sense of guilt over a lack of prevention.

The future inquiries would not find the security guards guilty of manslaughter or even negligent -there were too many protections because their work often required force.

It was yet another death in custody that could have been avoided. If she was dark-skinned or large in stature, Aino might have been targeted sooner and even more violently treated.

A renewed passion arose in Billy to build alternatives to psych wards. He initially wanted to destroy the institutions of health and policing that had punished so many people who were vulnerable and unwell. He then saw the growth of Well Tree as the construction of preventive pathways and alternatives to hospitals. Their careful construction might deconstruct the worst parts of the currently broken public institutions.

At his local supermarket, Billy bumped into the Peer Worker Mark from the hospital. Mark was trying to fix the many cracks in the system from the inside using his past experiences as a patient to advocate for change. It was not the same dynamic seeing

Mark outside of the hospital as if Billy had been met with professional barriers that doctors and nurses might put up.

During their quick chat in the veggie aisle, Billy admired Mark's efforts to change the system from within despite how slow this would. Mark admired Billy's innovative app and offered a few ideas.

"You should speak to Jason at HealWork, they have a platform you build into your app to save time" suggested Mark while scribbling down his contact's email address. It was like Mark was a matchmaker as Jason and Billy were kindred spirits. The HealWork platform had a lot of the data needed to suggest treatment options and had a massive user base that they were prepared to share because their non-profit mission aligned completely with Well Tree. In exchange for the integration work, full license to use the platform and access to all user data, HealWork would get 70 hotdesks in The Factory for two years to start in early 2021.

Before the proposed partnership was offered to HealWork, Billy got permission from his employer for Well Tree to sublease the space and create a PR opportunity for the three-way partnership. The plan for next year would be for an exec or co-founder to come with a couple of tech and creative arts journalists to unveil a large Osprey sculpture in front of The Factory with the name Aino engraved into a large brass plaque.

Billy felt bad switching on video streaming after the terrible news of Aino's death. He needed a distraction and had missed several series while in hospital. His oversized TV and soundbar streamed his new guilty pleasure with the much-talked-about line:

> "Do you know why animals die in cages? It's because their souls die."

~ 20 ~

TWENTY

Jacob woke up one day in mid-December very glad that much of the terror of the pandemic seemed to now be behind Australia. Liverpool had been the reddest of red zones with so many clusters popping up in neighbouring suburbs.

Jacob wondered whether this was a test. Looking at the cluster data from the Health Department website, there appeared to be some sort of epicentre in South West Sydney that Jacob was suspicious of. Tests of sewage water had recently found traces of the virus with warnings going out to 40 suburbs nearby. Then one of the quarantine workers who lived in the South West but worked in a medi-hotel in the city caught Covid.

Jacob masked up even though most people in the area had stopped using them. He went down to the large shopping mall and had a familiar but strange sense of some invisible barrier between his mind and the world. He felt a disconnect from the land he was walking on but somehow still tuned-in to messages from someone trying to tell him something.

At the shopping mall, the music in the centre's main speakers switched from Christmas carols to a song called Sweet Like Chocolate. Jacob thought this was a message to buy Cherry some of her favourite white chocolate. Though the thought itself was not normal, having the thought was not dangerous and did not require an admission. Even acting on this particular thought would be totally innocent, but one of Jacob's voices made him interpret the song differently -as something about his skin not being chocolate colour.

Jacob was becoming very unwell again but luckily, he had private health insurance and told Cherry about this set of thoughts which seemed logical to him but unusual to her. Cherry arranged an admission taking over four hours to find a private psych ward with a bed and arranging the GP appointment to get the required referral letter.

"You've got this relapse really early Jacob" said Dr Phan. "You are lucky to have someone who you trust to share your thoughts with. You are also one of only a few of my patients who can afford private health cover" the doctor continued.

The private psychiatric system would still not be an option if Jacob was in extreme crisis -they just can't accept people presenting too many risks or with highly acute symptoms.

The small ward at the Waterside Private Clinic had some very interesting characters. There were several veterans of the defence forces who experience PTSD. There was also a young Lesbian woman who had first been hospitalised in late 2017 after internalising a lot of the hateful debate around the Australian Marriage Law Postal Survey.

The veterans were of different ages but had similarly dated attitudes to nationalism, racial diversity and masculinity. Even the female veterans were masculinised by their past defence roles which made it difficult for them to talk openly about their emotions -especially not to 'civvies' (civilians).

Though they had less resources than the public hospital in terms of allied health staff like dieticians, social workers and occupational therapists, the nurses were friendly and more present on the ward than in the public system. There was also more of a consumer dynamic which pretended to be responsive to consumer needs but was still highly profit focused. If the pursuit of profit brings better outcomes for patients, Jacob was not that bothered with how corporate the place was.

The food was excellent and group programs highly structured. While not the utopia that everyone needs to get better, the fewer restrictions on things like mobile phones certainly seemed like major improvements compared to most public psych wards.

Jacob saw a new psychiatrist at Waterside three times a week. This doctor was not a junior Registrar like in public, but an experienced Consultant.

Dr Babu and his new patient joked a lot, but Jacob just found the jokes inappropriate and belittling. Would this Doctor go on Jacob's Target List?

That evening, a mix of patients all smoked cigarettes out in the garden under a large gazebo they called the 'dome of wisdom'. A lot of wisdom about life and mental distress was indeed shared there with many tears shed under that roof. Five patients in the dome saw Jacob on the other side of the garden and seemed like they were talking about him.

"He's schizo, not like the PTSD and depression of the rest of us" Jacob seemed to hear from an old veteran of the Vietnam war. Jacob wasn't sure if he could trust his senses but his voices at the time (mis)interpreted what was said and encouraged him to act on what he heard. "They should all go on The List, they all deserve it" Jacob was told by a voice that was amplifying his own thought at that time.

With new meds, Jacob told Dr Babu that his voices quickly became manageable again. The second hospitalisation of the year would be less than two weeks. He could have stayed longer but he asked to leave as he had critical work to do before the year ended.

Jacob's phone now was also tracking his location and changes in his facial expression and tone in voice. Billy had quickly adapted some AI software used to detect pain in people's faces to assess mood disorders and signs of flat affect from psychotic disorders. Jacob's face and tone led to green lights – he trusted that he was good to leave hospital.

~ 21 ~

TWENTY-ONE

On a thundery summer day, Billy, Cherry and Jacob mourned over a newly interned grave. They had only known the newly deceased for part of that year, but it was still painful. She had brought joy into their hearts -especially for Billy at his loft. She had a troubled early life and her suffering ended quickly without much pain.

Billy played two songs about death released that year by pop stars associated with the Bond franchise. The new movie was postponed to at least 2021. To Die for by Sam Smith and Billy No Time To Die by Billie Eilish were dramatic ways to send off this gentle soul. Billy and Jacob easily lifted the makeshift coffin into the ground -a final end to a troubled life peppered with happiness only at the end.

It could have easily been Jacob or one of their friends in that grave, but it was Billy's cat.

In 2020 so many Australians had adopted cats, dogs and other pets while they worked from home more. As they returned to work, these pets might feel neglected but more flexible work arrangements were inevitable now. It was a bit ridiculous how much importance animals had in the year's life narratives, but furry companions clearly had mental health benefits but also in created habits of care that gave purpose and new routines.

The threats of the bushfires to koalas had also been a major concern at the start of the year -perhaps more so than the mental health crisis.

The brain tumour that killed Y near the end of the year got a lot more sympathy from Billy's colleagues than his disclosure that he was hospitalised for complex mental distress that year.

As the soil of Billy's local park started to turn to mud, the rain on his cheek masked his tears. Though it seemed ridiculous to give a cat full burial rights with a carefully chosen playlist, it was a small taste of grief to remind everyone present how lucky Australia had been to avoid even more Covid deaths that year. A total of 907 was undeniably tragic and not yet properly memorialised but tiny compared with global numbers and was trending toward a constant figure of zero daily deaths for now.

There were many potential vaccines now but still so much death, pain and fear globally. With these emotional taxes, ongoing recessions would also incubate even worse mental illnesses and distressing environments. The world would never be the same with most people burned from the pandemic with only a hint of hope and renewal now visible.

Santa might bring an effective vaccine for Christmas or the parties and family events could lead to further infection throughout Western countries. The pandemic of suicidality could also peak with the pressures of family events and heightened loneliness felt by many over the holidays.

Using the holiday downtime to bring 12 diverse people together, Jacob sent out an invitation to three LGBTQI+ people, three war veterans, three indigenous people and three nurses. They were told they would get $200 for the time but without much explanation. The Factory was dimly lit that day with no one else there. He asked the twelve people he had seen that year to line up along one of the exposed brick walls which now had plastic painter's drop sheets hanging from it.

"This year I came across each of you and what happened filled me with anger. It also gradually triggered me to come up with a plan to bring you all together one day" Jacob said seriously.

"You each represent one of our top four most important groups to target with the pilot version of our new app. Improving wellness for people like you will be our biggest challenge and we need your ideas now to co-design our approach" said Jacob referring to a method of not just consulting with your users but having them design the services people like them will use in the future.

"So, we get $200 for a focus group" said one of the nurses who really only thought in black and white. "No, it's a small gift and lunch to thank you for shaping services that will benefit your colleagues and your consumers" Jacob rebutted.

The four teams worked within their own sets of three for brainstorming but then the groups were mixed up to get richer ideas penned in permanent marker on the drop sheets on the wall. Jacob deeply listened to their ideas and feedback and allowed them to reshape his unspecific goals as long as they stuck to his overall vision.

The group was led through mindfulness activities and were given raffle tickets designed like game badges when they had good ideas or built on the ideas of others. The mood score of the group was compared with the artificial intelligence in the new app in terms of whether the scanned micro-expressions of group member faces aligned with their self-reported mood. It was closely aligned with the reported score except when the user was masking problems with their mood with a deliberately higher score.

The nurses were intrigued by all the technology but found it most difficult to think beyond current systems, structures and restraints. Jacob tried to reframe their efforts using a question inspired by Nobel Laureate Economist Amartya Sen:

> "If you could rebuild the mental health system, how would you give people in mental distress the freedom to choose how they live their lives with meaning and purpose?"

Each participant was given their cash after a nice lunch and one person won a Christmas hamper in the raffle.

On Christmas Day, Jacob and Cherry's guests were almost as diverse as the co-design group. Billy, Aroha, Jessie, Jacob and Cherry had a tough year but were blessed with this new chosen family to spend the holidays with.

It did not seem right to celebrate the New Year at Sydney's scaled-back fireworks after the year the city had. Instead, the new family of five all went to Billy's loft and had drinks with his neighbours including Ted in the back shared courtyard. A massive watermelon and strawberry cake was served to everyone with a big 21 piped onto it -a postponed tribute to Billy's 21st in March.

"10-9-8-7-6-5-4-3-2-1" they all screamed together with each second bringing more relief that 2020 was over. This relief was tainted slightly by fears of relapse and new waves of infection in 2021.

Their journeys flowed in bold new directions and 2020 was just a temporary diversion for lives destined to foster the greater good.

Epilogue

With the borders now reopened to New Zealand, the trio were reunited in Queenstown. The mountain town in summer was a perfect temperature for Jessie to avoid getting too sweaty and feeling gross. A diverse bunch of 36 came to the wedding -all glad to be finally out of Australia for a celebration then holiday.

Jessie and Lachlan were married in a cute gazebo in Queenstown Gardens. Jessie entered along a dirt pathway in a vintage ivory wedding dress. No blood relatives were there for Jessie but all of her true family were present. Even those she lost from overdose or suicide were there in spirit and in her memory.

Billy wore a rainbow pin *in memoriam* for all same sex couples who couldn't get married before 2017 brought a change in the marriage laws in Australia.

Jacob and Cherry held their half-Taiwanese daughter whose cheeky spew on Jacob's trigonometry tie foreshadowed his hangover after an epic reception.

Billy walked Jessie down the aisle as *A Thousand Years* played on acoustic guitar. It was an fitting choice of song to get married to after 2020 given it contrasted death with eternal love. The waves of death and disease still had rippled across the world and both Australia and New Zealand had not felt the worst of them.

Despite being born in New Zealand, Lachlan did not know much about Maori customs or specifics like the health system there. Jessie looked around the lake, ski cabins and mountains and felt she was in a version of Western Lapland that had been localised to suit Aussies and Kiwis. The country still carried with it remains of Maori cultural wisdom that were strong enough to survive colonisation.

A basic but large tent with vintage charm had been erected along part of the lake. As the semi-formally dressed guests arrived, Jessie and Lachlan were greeted with warmth that they could draw from for the rest of their lives. There were circus acts to match the circus tent-like setting and a drag queen to bring the night together and try and stop the six-member band from going to the bar so often.

An old upright piano sat along the edge of the temporary dance floor. A few champagnes into the night, the music stopped. Jessie worried someone might have tripped over the haphazard cords of the speakers or a band member had passed out drunk. Jessie looked around to see Lachlan at the piano where he started to play *River Flows in You* so beautifully that Jessie wept.

She was not one to cry normally even with all the past pain in her life and did not cry at the service even when she saw Lachlan's eyes start to gloss over like a precursor to tears. It was like her past trauma was dripping out of her as the song was sombre and sad in tempo but ending in a higher pitch as a sign of hope. Her trauma wouldn't ever be washed away but she could see a strange beauty in sadness and it was like sad tears of past pain dripped from her left eye but happy tears of hope and pride in Lachlan dripped from her right eye.

Billy cringed at the song remembering it as a lullaby in a one of the Twilight vampire movies. He didn't believe in happily ever after and had no interest in getting married or even committing to dating people from a single gender.

Jessie deserved this moment and with the amazing weather and perfect ceremony, it was like Jessie was finally getting some good luck to balance out so many years of emotional torture. She was being rewarded with Lachlan by some karmic force on top of plain serendipity and a tweaked dating app algorithm. As Lachlan's bony fingers skipped passed the last few keys of the piano, he tapped his phone which started a drum and bass backing track he produced to mash up with faster playing of the lullaby.

Like the circus tent hosting her wedding reception, Jessie and her new hubby Lachlan's life would not be in any one fixed position. They would rebuild their life wherever they travelled and would find new people to support them in exchange for plenty of support back. Jessie would move to find her next Billy with Lachlan's love supporting her just enough so she could look after herself first, then others. She would have enough energy left over to look after Lachlan and the new people she crossed paths with who needed direction.

Jessie glanced out at the reflections of the mountain on the lake and thought how the early experiences in the Blue Mountains might have been getting her fit and ready for guiding others. She didn't wish the pain and dangers of these experiences on anyone. She had been so close to cliff edges and every moment of stepping back from the edge was a relief that gave her strength to keep climbing up and guiding others up behind her.

The trip had made most of the guests anxious about their own potential relapse or the relapse of those they care for. It was terrible to live their life that way but at least this meant they had crisis plans updated and ready. Travelling from West to East for long distances combined with jet lag has been found to trigger mania in a small cohort of people with bipolar but the short trip eastward across the ditch did not have the same risk.

The act of travel and time to reflect on the plane made Billy, Jessie and Jacob all reflect on the flow of their lives and where they were headed now. They were all in better positions to rebound from relapse, but Jacob still considered his own mortality. He was a father now so had more to live for but imagined the possibility of one day being a burden to his wife and daughter.

A referendum had just made euthanasia legal in New Zealand. For people who were terminally ill given only six months to live, two doctors could authorise assisted dying. Jacob wondered if his weight gain, cognitive impairments and intensity of voices would one day be sufficient grounds for euthanasia like they were in a handful of cases in the Netherlands.

While the main Well Tree execs were all in New Zealand, a re-fit of The Factory was being managed by Aroha. Acrylic panels created an artificial clear ceiling and set of moveable walls. The pods were totally sealed with aluminium slotting into a gasketed ceiling grid. The temporary modular system could create overnight accommodation or potentially negative pressure isolation rooms for quarantining.

There was still much to be done to address the fallout of 2020 and prepare for the next crisis.

Afterword

This is not a *Roman à clef* in a traditional sense. The characters are segments or combinations of people and the façade of fiction overlaying true events is itself grounded in real world facts. As such, fact bleeds into fiction.

The confluence of the journeys of Billy, Jessie and Jacob is where my own story lies, and an understanding of which parts have been fictionalised may remain a mystery.

I encourage you to tell your own story authentically but with twists or omissions to protect your audience and yourself. If reading this story or telling your own story triggers any issues for you, get professional help quickly starting with your GP or helplines on the United for Global Mental Health website (quick link at: tayar.com.au/h).

Mark Tayar, PhD
December 2020

www.ingramcontent.com/pod-product-compliance
Lightning Source LLC
Chambersburg PA
CBHW071922130726
47909CB00014B/2511